Carrie sudde

There was someone nearby, a footstep on the clay tiles behind her. Carrie ran—ran for her life.

A hand reached out and grabbed her wrist, spun her back and into a wall of heated muscle. Powerful arms encircled her, pressed her body close to his.

She knew the smell, sensed the safety, sobbed out his name. "Alex."

Hot lips scored hers in a frenzy of passion. The whole desperate night rushed in on her and she clung to him, her breasts heaving with exertion, her mouth burning with a need.

"Dear God!" he rasped at last, his voice coming from deep within his throat. "If you must tear barefoot through the night like a wild gypsy you'll have to suffer the consequences."

NATALIE FOX was born and educated in London. She's had many interesting careers, including working in a casino as a roulette croupier, and working for a Soho coffee bar, for which she delivered sandwiches by scooter in the West End. Although she didn't start writing until after her fortieth birthday, Natalie says she's, "always been a romantic at heart." Natalie and her husband now live in Spain.

NATALIE FOX

nights of desire

Harlequin Books

TORONTO • NEW YORK • LONDON
AMSTERDAM • PARIS • SYDNEY • HAMBURG
STOCKHOLM • ATHENS • TOKYO • MILAN
MADRID • WARSAW • BUDAPEST • AUCKLAND

Harlequin Presents first edition July 1992
ISBN 0-373-11473-7

Original hardcover edition published in 1991
by Mills & Boon Limited

NIGHTS OF DESIRE

CHAPTER ONE

CARRIE SUTHERLAND had never chased a man in her life, until now. And what a way to do it!

'I'm not doing this!' Carrie breathed to herself as the Marina del Oro helicopter whisked her down over the shoreline, hugging the beach where bronzed holidaymakers languished under the hot Spanish sun.

Howard was down there somewhere, she mused, gazing out of the window. Not lazing in the sun but more than likely closing a deal with delighted clients buying a piece of paradise in the sun. She hadn't been happy about Howard taking this job and as was her way she had voiced her disapproval.

'Don't you ever read the Sunday papers?' she had argued. 'Time-share has a bad press...'

'There's time-share and time-share, sweetheart. Puerto del Sol has a good reputation and, let's face it, nothing can be worse than being out of work in London all summer. I might as well be down in southern Spain doing something I'm good at and earning money.' He'd slid his arms around her waist. 'I'll miss you like crazy, darling, but it's only for the season.'

'But Howard, something will turn up here if you just have a bit of patience. You've only been out of work for a month.'

'A month too long,' Howard had said bitterly.

Howard's pride had taken a beating when the company he had worked for had merged with another and he had been one of the unfortunates who had been surplus to requirements. It had affected him badly. He'd grown depressed and irritable, his moods rubbing off on Carrie.

'I do understand how you feel, Howard, but six months apart...' She hadn't been able to finish, to even hint that the time apart might ruin their already shaky relationship.

He'd brushed his lips along her jawline. 'I know, sweetheart, it will be miserable, but if we want to get married next year...' He'd gripped her shoulders, almost fiercely. 'You do still want to marry me, don't you?'

Even now she couldn't recall what she had said to that. She cared very deeply for Howard, but was it strong enough for marriage? In a way Carrie was almost grateful for the collapse of Howard's job. It had shown her a side of him she might never have seen till it was too late. His bitterness was understandable but his 'the world owes me' attitude wasn't. But the months apart had taken their toll on her; she felt guilty for having doubts about her future with him. She needed to see him to be sure.

Then fate had intervened and given her a golden opportunity. Her own job had suddenly been threatened. Tenson's were moving up north and Carrie wasn't prepared to leave London to go with them, so she had signed on with an agency and the first job they'd offered her was personal secretary to a financier in the City. Nothing terribly thrilling in that, but her first two months with the company would be spent on the Costa del Sol. That was thrilling!

Those two months had clinched it for Carrie, especially when she'd found that the new development the financier Alexander Drayton was pouring money into was in the same province as Howard's company. She'd find him, reassure herself one way or the other. If that wasn't destiny for you, what was?

Being transported to her new job by helicopter was certainly an impressive start, Carrie mused. Let's hope Drayton lived up to expectations. She hadn't had the pleasure of meeting him yet. He'd been unavoidably delayed in Switzerland when her interview had come up and Carrie had been taken on by his outgoing secretary, a very married, very pregnant lady.

The sun worshippers grew thin on the shore as the helicopter headed east from Malaga airport, the coastline changing dramatically from unspectacular beaches to spectacular craggy coves where the Mediterranean frothed furiously against outcrops of rock.

She glanced down as the pilot gestured out of the window, her excitement bubbling as the helicopter whirred down low over clear blue water and swept into a cool white marina.

Carrie got a swift impression of bright white villas, terracotta roofs and gleaming sea craft moored at berths that jutted into the calm harbour, and another impression of luxuriant subtropical landscape, turquoise sea and deep blue sky as the helicopter landed with a bump on a concrete pad adjoining pink tennis courts.

'Caroline Sutherland? Welcome to Marina del Oro. My name is Adela Carmen Rivera. I hope your journey was satisfactory.'

Carrie was met by a stunning Spanish lady, her English so good that there was scarcely an accent but delivered with such cold emotion Carrie didn't feel welcome at all. She was so coolly elegant that she made travel-weary Carrie feel decidedly scruffy.

'The flight was fine,' Carrie replied cheerily, following her to an open-topped car emblazoned with the same company logo as the helicopter: Marina del Oro. The pilot loaded her suitcase into the boot and Adela Rivera sped off without a backward glance at the pilot who gave Carrie a wink and a wave.

'I show you to your apartment and then tell Alex you're here.' Adela said stiffly.

Alex, eh? Carrie wondered where the striking woman featured in *his* life. She wasn't wife material, that was for sure. She looked career-minded, more capable of running this new development than a home. Maybe she did. Drayton was only the money after all. Carrie tried to study her without appearing to. She had similar colouring to her own, dark eyes and clear olive skin, glossy dark hair spun into a sophisticated coil at the nape of her neck whereas Carrie's blew wildly in the wind.

The apartment was way beyond Carrie's expectations.

'Oh, it's beautiful!' she gasped, thinking she probably sounded gauche.

'*Everything* on the Marina del Oro is beautiful,' Adela clipped. Her tone was so uppity that it raised the hairs on the back of Carrie's neck.

Including yourself, no doubt, Carrie thought uncharitably.

'This is one of the smaller apartments. Intended only for weekend use, of course.' But it's OK to put me in here for the duration, Carrie thought with amusement. 'You will be shown the rest of the development later, after you have showered and refreshed yourself.'

'Good grief, do I look that bad?' Carrie peered at herself in the mirror after Adela had left.

She did look somewhat jaded, she agreed regretfully. Her chestnut hair tumbled chaotically around her shoulders and faint shadows under her dark brown eyes reminded her she had hardly slept a wink last night. The thought of meeting up with Howard again had confused sleep from her mind.

She ached for a shower but first inspected the apartment. The floors were white marble throughout for coolness, the furniture light cane upholstered in pastel colours. Cool green blinds arched out over the terrace which ran the length of the apartment from lounge to bedroom.

Carrie slid open the patio doors and stepped outside. She was on the first floor, just one apartment above her.

It was July and hot but a breeze from the sea made it comfortable. The terrace overlooked the marina and Carrie thought if she stood there for ever she would never cease to wonder at it. She wasn't a boat person but no one could deny their beauty. Sleek, sophisticated, millions of pounds' worth of elegance roped to the quayside.

The apartment had a sitting-room with a raised dining area. There was a streamlined kitchen equipped with every device to relieve the chore of cooking. Carrie wasn't a great cook and Howard grumbled that she ought to be more imaginative but she usually managed to produce something edible. You could produce a banquet with all these aids, she mused, running her fingers over marble worktops.

Howard, she thought. There had been no time to contact him to tell him she was coming and she was glad of that. He would probably have insisted on meeting her at the airport and she wasn't prepared for that yet. Strange country, new job. She needed time to settle.

She unpacked quickly and took a long shower in the marbled bathroom, reminding herself to phone her father to say she had arrived safely.

Carrie's mother had died when Carrie was fourteen; she had taken on her father's well-being and loved him dearly. He wasn't like other fathers— Tate Sutherland lived in a strange world of ancient coins and medals, a passion she would have liked to share if she had had more time. He wrote books on numismatics that probably only ten people in the world would benefit from and had a fabulous collection of oriental coins which occasionally he was forced to trade with to pay the bills. But things had been easier since Carrie had left secretarial college; she was a first-class secretary and earned good money.

'Oh, my God!' Carrie shrieked, frantically swinging the towel coiled round her wet hair to cover her nakedness. She'd gone into the sitting-room for her bag and got *the* shock of her life. 'What do you want?' she screeched. 'My money?

Take it!' She jerked her head towards the bag. 'Take it and get out!'

He said nothing at first, just stood looking her up and down, taking it all in. The towel trembling around her thighs, water drizzling from her chestnut hair to her bare shoulders, puddles forming at her feet. He spoke at last and Carrie died!

'Alexander Drayton. Pleased to meet you, Miss Sutherland.'

He could have smiled, shown some spark of humour to ease her cringing embarrassment. Nothing. With cold calculation he extended a hand in greeting.

She *couldn't* take it, though what did it matter if the towel slipped? He'd seen it all, *everything*!

He dropped his hand to his side. 'I'll leave you to dress. Perhaps when I come back your colour will have returned to normal,' he said flintily, and shut the door quietly behind him.

Carrie fled back to the bathroom where she locked herself in and nearly wept in misery. How could that have happened? What a start! She'd thought him a burglar, practically thrown her money at him, *and* she'd been naked at the time!

Minutes later her face was still flushed, her brown eyes still bright with shock. So that was Alexander Drayton, was it? For the life of her she couldn't bring his face back to her tortured senses. She'd been aware of darkness and height, yet every feature of his face eluded her now.

She dressed quickly in case he came back, in a cool linen dress guaranteed not to offend. She combed through her wet hair but had no time to dry it before he tapped on the door.

'I'm sorry,' she humbled as she opened it. 'You caught me unawares before——'

'I did knock but you were obviously under the shower and the door wasn't locked.' He gave the impression he thought it her fault.

Bravely Carrie extended her hand to his. He took it without a smile, seemed to look through her to her bones. Carrie felt smaller than her five feet six, in stature and significance.

He carried papers; that was the first thing she noticed about him—the next was his eyes. So very dark and penetrating. Almost suspicious. It didn't surprise her. Men who dealt in money always looked cautious to her, as if everyone was out to con them. Her not so friendly bank manager at home had the same look about him!

Alexander Drayton was autocratic, no denying that, he had to be in his world, but it was inbred not acquired. His accent suggested an expensive education and a privileged upbringing. He wasn't a self-made man—his ex-secretary had told Carrie he came from wealthy stock—and yet the power he emanated gave Carrie the feeling he'd be a success in whatever field he approached. In a lighter vein Carrie judged him to be a man who ate muesli for breakfast, drove a dependable Rover and never made a mistake in his life. He was good-looking, not handsome.

Carrie's thoughts switched to Howard. Now Howard *was* handsome. Golden-haired, outgoing Howard, who had used to laugh so easily. Did this Drayton man ever laugh or even smile?

Her new employer flicked through the papers in his hand, selected one and placed it neatly on top of the others.

'Sit down, will you?' he said quietly and took a seat across from her in the sitting-room.

This was beginning to feel like an interview. Carrie sat obediently with her hands in her lap.

'I see you were three years with Tenson Import and Export. Personal secretary to Sir Michael Spiers. Why did you leave?'

His question was unexpected. She presumed he was reading through her CV. A bit late in the day; his outgoing secretary had already interviewed and hired her.

'They were moving from London to Northumbria and I wasn't prepared to move with them,' she answered.

'It was a good position. Your references are impeccable. It was obvious they didn't want to lose you.' His eyes penetrated hers until, not able to stand it any longer, she studied a point above his head through a fringe of lashes. 'Family ties?' he added.

'Yes, I live with my father and look after him. I didn't want to leave him.'

'You've left him now,' he said accusingly.

'I . . .' Carrie felt her neck flush. She squashed the irritation his questions aroused in her. 'Your company is based in London, in the City, and your secretary assured me this part of the job, here in Spain, was only temporary. My father isn't the sort to stand in my way and assured me he could manage for a while without me.'

No way could she tell him that this was the part of the job that had decided her. She needed this time on the Costa to sort out her feelings for Howard, and Mrs Burbage next door had promised to cook her father a hot meal every day and to keep an eye on him.

'How long did my secretary say you would be here?' His eyes narrowed beneath dark brows.

'About two months.'

'And suppose it's six?'

'I . . . I hadn't thought.'

'It could be less. You might not suit me,' he told her arrogantly.

Carrie gripped her fingers tightly. And *you* might not suit me Mr High and Mighty Drayton, she thought, but she said nothing.

'My references are in order, I believe,' she murmured.

'Faultless. But your personality might not suit.'

I'm being goaded, Carrie thought angrily, but I'm not going to argue.

He seemed slightly perturbed by her silence, which surprised Carrie. She didn't think he was capable of being ruffled.

He lowered his dark eyes to the sheet of paper again. 'It says here you speak Spanish. How did that come about?' He said it in Spanish and that annoyed Carrie more than the disbelief of his tone. He was testing her.

'I studied for it,' she told him fluently. 'And had reason to use it when dealing with clients in my last position.'

He nodded, satisfied, and resumed speaking in their native tongue. 'You realise there will be a trial period of employment.'

She hadn't realised at all! His secretary had mentioned no such conditions. She narrowed her deep brown eyes at him, studied the top of his head as he flicked through more papers. His hair was as black as coal, straight and sleek, not a hair out of place. I don't like you, she thought with a jolt, and I don't think for a minute I'm going to like working for you! Huh, who was she kidding? She might never get the chance. It was obvious he thought his ex-secretary had made an unfortunate choice for her replacement.

He stood up, towered over her as she shakily got to her feet, the inquisition over. 'A trial period to see if we can scratch along together,' he went on. 'I'm not easy to work for. I expect perfection. I *demand* perfection.' He reached out and tilted her chin upwards. 'You might have the perfect body, Miss Sutherland, but let's see if your other talents come up to expectations.'

He left her fuming in the middle of the room but turned at the carved oak door, nearly catching her pulling a face at his retreating back. 'I'll be back in an hour to take you over the development and show you where you will be working.'

When he'd gone Carrie flung herself down on the sofa, pummelling a cushion to release her anger. Damn him! He was *awful*!

She blow-dried her thick hair, tamed the deep waves into a sleek curtain of dark satin. She'd show him. She'd prove she was twice the secretary her glowing references claimed she was. He wouldn't find fault with her; she wouldn't give him the chance! It was as she applied a gloss to her full lips, a coating of mascara to her lashes, that she wondered why she felt the need to prove anything at all.

Exactly an hour later Alexander Drayton pulled up outside the apartments. He tooted his horn, a gesture which mildly surprised Carrie. She hurried down and slid into the passenger seat of his air-conditioned Mercedes.

'We'll start at the marina and work our way back up through the development. Ask questions. I want you to be familiar with every aspect of the Marina del Oro.' He drove on, not looking at her, eyes ahead.

'It's very beautiful,' Carrie commented after a while as they cruised slowly along the quayside. 'Do you have a . . . a boat?' Should she have said yacht?

'Sailing holds no interest for me whatsoever,' he told her drily. 'I'm only concerned with the development giving a good return for my investment.'

Carrie said no more. She wondered where his leisure interests lay—the same place as his business interests no doubt, turning base metal to gold with one look of those piercing monetary eyes!

At the far end of the marina he pulled up, and parked outside a white building that stood alone. They got out of the car.

'This is where we will be working. The administration centre.' To her surprise he took her elbow, and guided her away from the building. 'But first I'll show you around the completed first phase of apartments and villas.'

Alexander Drayton was in no hurry and Carrie was grateful for that. As they walked he talked, and she listened. The afternoon heat was heavy and debilitating. Her discomfort was soon forgotten though as they strolled through shady passages linking the luxurious accommodation. Each unit was individually designed, villas and town houses built to moorish design.

Drayton pointed out the many features that made the architecture so fascinating. Handmade bricks of pink and white, antique roof tiles subtly blended with the new, pretty wrought-iron grilles and flowers cascading from every balcony and rampaging over every natural stone wall.

'It's all been built to recreate an authentic Spanish village,' he explained, 'with the added advantage of up-to-date facilities for the discerning sailing enthusiast.' He sounded like the Marina del Oro blurb his London secretary had given her to read.

'It's all quite exquisite,' Carrie breathed at last.

'So why are you frowning?' he asked unexpectedly, and Carrie jerked her head to look at him, surprised that he had noticed. They had stopped by a cool fountain in a small courtyard and Carrie reached out to let the spray trickle over her wrists.

'There's something wrong,' she answered hesitantly, averting her eyes.

'With the villas, the gardens?'

Carrie shook her head, smoothed a curtain of silky hair from her cheek with the back of her hand. 'The place is very lovely. Superbly designed. No one could fault that, but...' She shrugged her narrow shoulders, wondering if she should be so outspoken.

'Go on,' he urged impatiently.

She looked at him then, still not sure what to say. His impatience irritated her and she knew if she was to work for him for long she would probably get ulcers. He appeared the sort to demand her opinion simply for the pleasure of overruling it.

Taking a courageous breath, Carrie went on, 'It's dead, the only life the bees on that hibiscus over there. It's like some obsolete film set.'

'No players to act out our fantasies,' he murmured after a long pause.

Carrie was surprised by such a comment and her eyes flicked up to catch his. He was studying her so intently that she looked away quickly. She had a feeling of being trapped in a vacuum of scented flowers, soft trickling water and something that was so positively sensual that her heart raced unexpectedly.

'Yes,' he clipped suddenly, evaporating the heady atmosphere. 'No people. Bad marketing. The majority of these units are empty, unsold. The timeshare units did well but not well enough to save the company. I wasn't involved in this first phase. But I'm here now to inject money and life into the next.'

He went on to explain the collapse of the original company involved in the marina as they continued their tour of inspection and Carrie struggled to concentrate. He had aroused her curiosity. He didn't seem the sort to fantasise. He was as smooth, cool and impersonal as the marble that was used abundantly here. Even his clothes were unsensational, a crisp white short-sleeved shirt and knife-edged narrow black trousers. He wore a tie, in this heat he wore a tie!

'We've started work on the equestrian section and the country club is well under way. There's a swimming pool behind our apartments. Take advantage of it whenever you can; there will be little time for recreation in the next weeks.'

Our apartments! Did he live here too? How could she swim and relax with him around?

They arrived back at the admin. centre and went inside.

'As you see, the ground floor is devoted to sales.' He waved a hand towards aerial shots of the marina and surroundings displayed on the walls of the reception area. There were squashy sofas and masses of greenery in terracotta pots. A scale model of the completed project stood between a desk and the window.

Alexander Drayton stood by it, and pointed out the planned new phases, four in all. As he stretched over the model, muscles bunched within his shirt, Carrie wondered if the unseen flesh was as dark and tanned as the skin of his face and arms.

'Are you all right? You look very pale.' The soft timbre of his voice actually sounded concerned.

'It's a little warm, that's all,' she murmured, astonished that she had paled at the thought of what lay beneath his shirt. The sun must have gone to her head.

'We'll have a drink when we get upstairs. I'd advise you to take plenty of fluids in this heat, otherwise you won't be capable of working at full capacity.'

Of course, one must be fit enough to work at full capacity! I will, don't worry, Carrie determined to herself as they took the stairs to the next floor.

'And in case you are wondering where the staff are, we close for siesta from two till five. Usually there is someone on duty in Reception but we have a staff problem at present. You might be roped in to do a stint if we can't find someone permanent. Do you object to that?' He led the way along an airy corridor, not pausing for her answer.

'I'll do it if I must but I'm not a sales person——'

'Quite,' he clipped.

'This is your office.' He flung open a door, crossed the room and flung open another. 'And this is mine.'

The two offices were intimately segregated from the rest of the office suites on that floor. This was Alexander Drayton's domain. Lush carpeting, mahogany furnishings, essential air-conditioning. Her own office was a watered-down version of his, impressive nevertheless. Equipped with everything to guarantee the smooth running of his financial empire.

'Now, before we do anything else I'd like you to read through this contract and sign it if you are happy with your terms of employment. I'll pour you a drink.' He left her in the outer office and Carrie picked up the document, her eyes widening with shock as she flashed through it.

The salary was far higher than his secretary had quoted. Mind you, she was going to have to work her fingers to the bone for it. Alexander Drayton might be generous but his demands were high. No set hours and on call at all times, day and night.

He was entitled to dismiss her on the spot whereas she was compelled to give a month's notice, all this of course after her month's trial period. Knowing the man as she did, the contract didn't surprise her at all. Carrie picked up a pen from her desk and signed away the last month of her twenty-fourth year.

'Where's Alex?' Adela clipped, and, not waiting for a reply, strutted past Carrie into Drayton's office, slamming the door behind her.

Carrie was intrigued to hear raised voices, sadly not clear enough to discern what the row was about. Not nosy by nature, Carrie would have made an exception this time. Anything to gain insight into what made the grim Alexander Drayton tick.

Suddenly the door flew open and with lips thinned by repressed fury the Spanish beauty swept out. In the next instant Carrie heard, 'Miss Sutherland, will you come in here, please?'

She stepped into his office, her contract clutched in her hand. She closed the door behind her as his eyes motioned her to. He was standing with his back to the window and she could hardly see his face in the shadow but she sensed the fury. Whatever the row was about, Drayton was equally as angry as Rivera.

'You've made your first mistake.'

A chill ran down Carrie's spine.

'In future, no one, but no one gets past your office to mine, do you understand? My time is precious and I expect you to run a tight appointments schedule. I see no one without an appointment—is that clear?'

'Yes... yes, of course...' she uttered meekly.

'And that's your second mistake.' He stepped round his desk, stood close to her. She smelt his warmth. Unease spread through her like a bush fire. 'I can't stand subservience, Miss Sutherland.'

'Sub... subservience?'

'You know what it means, don't you?' he grated sarcastically.

Anger nudged aside her fear. Who the devil did he think he was? Just because he'd had a row with his mistress... his mistress? How had she come to that conclusion?

'Yes, of course,' she replied, biting her bottom lip. She couldn't work for this man, she just couldn't! By the end of the month she'd be an emotional cripple!

'It's not good enough, Miss Sutherland.' His eyes narrowed and a pulse at his jaw throbbed deeply.

'What's not good enough?' she asked, clenching her fists to try and restrain herself. Whatever had *she* done to bring all this on?

'I don't think we are going to get on at all, Miss Sutherland,' he told her slowly and with deliberation.

His eyes never left hers and then Carrie saw the light. This had nothing to do with a lovers' tiff. He simply didn't think her qualifications were up to his demands. Well, to hell with him!

She had the contract right here in her hand and she knew exactly what she would like to tell him to do with it! Instead she crunched it tightly in two hands, only inches from his face.

'I'll save you the trouble of firing me before I start, Mr Drayton. Take this as my resignation.' She ripped it apart, flung it to the floor. 'I can't work for a man who is unreasonable——'

'Is it unreasonable to expect my secretary to keep undesirables from my door?' He raised a mocking brow.

Adela was an undesirable, was she? Carrie could bet she hadn't always been.

'Your personal life has nothing to do with me. I was hired to work for you, not to keep women out of your bed!'

His dark eyes narrowed dangerously. She'd gone too far and knew it, but what did it matter? She had nothing more to lose. 'I don't like you enough to want to fight for this job,' she blazed on. 'I'm good at my work, Mr Drayton and this loss is yours, I assure you. You wouldn't get anyone else to sign that ridiculous contract of yours. I'm leaving. Now!' She turned to the door, but never reached it. His hand locked around her tiny wrist.

'You're going nowhere. Did you sign that contract?'

Carrie didn't struggle in his grip—he'd have loved that, grappling with a defenceless female—but she defied him with the tilt of her chin, the fierceness of her eyes. 'Yes, I signed it. Are you going to hold me to it?' Though it lay crumbled and torn on the carpet she guessed he had the power to enforce it if he wished. Let him try!

'No, but I'm curious to know why you agreed to my somewhat harsh terms of employment. Was it the money?' There was a smirk on his lips and Carrie felt like slapping it away.

'Being a high-flying financier, I suppose, you be-lieve that everyone's allegiance has a price? Yes, you pay well, Mr Drayton, and so you should for the hours you demand, but the whole world is not motivated by money. Working abroad as your secretary, I would expect to be on call, night and day. I'm a conscientious worker and I don't down tools at five and leave a job half done. No, I don't find your *conditions* of employment objectionable, just you!'

With that she wrenched herself from him and stormed from the room. She got no further than the office she would have occupied if that man hadn't been such a moron.

'Get back in my office, Miss Sutherland.' He barred her way with a muscular brown arm across the doorway.

'No!' Her eyes blazed angrily. 'I've said all I have to say!'

'I damned well haven't!' he stormed. 'So get in my office before I half-nelson you in!'

Shocked, Carrie stared up at him. He would too. Head held high, she strode in front of him and stood to attention at his desk.

'Relax and join me in a drink. It's nearly six; I always take a dry Martini at this time.'

A dry Martini? After all that, was he serious? Hardly believing it, Carrie mumbled an acceptance. She watched in abject curiosity as he mixed the drinks at the bar across the room.

'I apologise if I upset you. I pushed you on purpose. If we are to work together we work on the same level.'

'I'm not sure I understand you.' Carrie murmured in a daze. What on earth was happening here?

'You hardly said a word all afternoon. I had to coax questions and answers from you. I know it's your first day but I haven't time to waste getting to know people. I've already seen you naked and that's that little mystery over with. I like to cut corners in relationships. We jell immediately or not at all. That's the way I run my life.'

He crossed the room, handed her her drink. Her mouth gaped open like that of a goldfish.

'I warn you I'm not easy to work with,' he went on, 'and I don't suffer fools gladly. When you work with me I expect you to voice an opinion, disagree if you feel so inclined, shout if you must, within reason of course. I've already judged you to be a person who won't abuse that privilege. Don't come running to me if your love-life goes awry but do come running to me with sensible suggestions on company policy. Do I make myself clear?'

She'd never met a man quite like this before, let alone worked for one. After all she had said to him he still wanted her. Then she understood. He wanted her *because* of what had just transpired. He was one of those dangerous breed of men who accepted women's equality, within reason of course!

'And what about me?' she asked defiantly. 'Suppose you don't jell for me?'

He stood so close to her now that she thought he must be able to see into her very soul. Her heart lurched unwillingly.

'I sign the pay cheques, Caroline,' he smoothed arrogantly.

How skilfully he had switched from formality to familiarity; it was Caroline now.

'That's your answer to everything is it—money?' she blurted hotly.

'Are you willing to work for nothing?' he retaliated.

'N...no...'

'What are you afraid of, then? If you wish to see *me* naked that can be easily arranged.'

For the first time she saw what passed as humour in his dark impenetrable eyes. She also saw danger with a capital 'D'. This man wasn't good-looking as she had first thought; he was devastating when the defences were down. They were down now.

'So you are staying?' he said when she didn't answer.

'Is that a question or a statement?' Carrie fired back over the rim of her glass.

He met her eyes with a look that filled Carrie with unease. 'I feel we will be good together,' was all he said on a smile, and turned away from her.

Carrie finished her drink in silence. Foreboding rattled its chains. This man with his innuendoes and his manipulative ways could be lethal. He would be an unconventional man to work for, at times probably insufferable, but one thing was for sure— he could never be boring.

With determination she reminded herself why she had taken the job in the first place. She had an uncomfortable feeling that working for Alexander Drayton might be more emotionally draining than deciding her future with Howard.

CHAPTER TWO

THERE was no time to dwell on that thought as Alexander Drayton machine-gunned her duties to Carrie over the next couple of hours and then, after plunging her in at the deep end with Adela Carmen Rivera and a pile of sales contracts, he picked up his car keys from the desk and said, 'I'll leave you two to get better acquainted. Don't keep Caroline too long, Adela; she must be nearing exhaustion.'

'Where are you going, Alex?' Adela asked crisply.

'Out, and no, I haven't forgotten our dinner engagement. I'll pick you up at ten.' With that he strode from the office.

So Carrie had been right. These two were romantically involved though there had been nothing romantic in the scowl on Drayton's face as he'd left and the catch in Adela's throat as he had snapped at her.

Adela was the company *abogada* and handled all the company's legal transactions as well as running her own legal consultancy. Carrie wasn't surprised. She was officious and Carrie could imagine her in the courtroom putting some poor soul down for life with a smile on her beautiful face.

Carrie hoped their paths wouldn't cross too often. If she hadn't taken to Adela, the feeling was mutual. Carrie could feel the hostility emanating from the woman though there was nothing definite to pin-point and no reason. Carrie was relieved when Adela wound up the session ten minutes later.

'I'll see you tomorrow.'

She walked out of the office, leaving Carrie drained. Exhaustion was an understatement.

She was in bed by ten, the witching hour when Alexander Drayton and Adela Rivera were going out to dine. I'll never get used to these strange hours of working, Carrie groaned into her pillow. She'd let herself into her apartment after nine. Someone had stocked the fridge with essentials and she'd scrambled some eggs and tumbled into bed to sleep forever.

She woke early, and decided a swim was a good thought, but aborted the idea when she found the pool already occupied. Standing behind a clump of oleanders, she watched in rapt curiosity. Yes, the rest of his body was the same copper as his face and arms, all over!

Carrie dragged her eyes away and scanned the windows of the other apartments surrounding the pool. All except two were shuttered, hers and the one directly above. She and Alexander Drayton were the only occupants of this part of the complex. No wonder he felt free to skinny-dip. The possibility of his naked form offending his secretary didn't merit a thought to him!

She showered instead of swam. Tried to get the image of his magnificent physique out of her head; tried to bring Howard's to mind. Howard. Today she must make enquiries and also phone her father.

'Mr Drayton, do you mind if I make a personal call from the office?'

He looked up from a pile of faxes she had just plopped on his desk.

'Boyfriend?' he asked, eyes narrowing.

'No. My father. I'd like to tell him I arrived safely. I was so tired last night that I forgot.'

'By all means.' His attention went back to his paperwork.

Carrie turned to go back to her own office.

'Call me Alex, not Mr Drayton,' he said behind her.

'Call me Carrie, not Caroline.' She closed the door behind her, convinced she hadn't imagined he'd chuckled.

Her father was well, pleased to hear she was settled and not at all bothered that she hadn't called the night before. If the truth was known, Carrie smiled as she put down the receiver, her father had probably been so deep in his catalogues that he didn't know what day it was anyway!

After her father Carrie gave thought to Howard. The sensible person to ask where the Puerto del Sol was would have been Alex. Alex—would she ever get used to calling him that? According to Adela he had secured finance for numerous leisure outlets along the Costa and knew the area well but she couldn't ask him and didn't really know why. Maybe the 'don't mix business and pleasure' syndrome or even the 'familiarity breeds contempt' one put her off. Though how much more familiar could one get with one's boss? Now she'd seen him naked too!

She decided the telephone book was the answer but pressure of work pushed the thought from her mind, until she made a strange discovery.

She'd gone along to the stationery room for envelopes and found a stack of headed paper—Puerto del Sol headed paper.

'Get rid of it,' Alex told her when she casually mentioned it.

'But what's it doing here?' If he thought her curiosity unusual he didn't say.

'It was the original name of the Marina del Oro...' Carrie felt her legs weaken. 'It went bust; undercapitalised, badly managed. I changed the staff and the name when I came in.'

Stunned, Carrie asked. 'How...how long ago was that?'

His curiosity was aroused now and Carrie hoped that uncontrollable blush of hers would stay away. 'Why do you want to know?' he asked, eyeing her through dark lashes.

Shrugging her shoulders she said, 'Just gathering more background.'

'Two months ago now——' The phone rang and he reached for it and she knew she would never be able to resume her line of questioning without arousing more suspicion. She left his office and sat in her own, too stunned to move.

Howard's last letter had arrived a month ago and there had been no mention of his losing his job, in fact he'd said things couldn't be better. Why had he lied, why hadn't he told her?

Her head ached for the rest of the day. She longed for siesta time but Alex didn't release her till gone three. Then she slumped on her bed, hot and restless.

Poor Howard. How could this happen to him a second time? It just wasn't fair. But where was he now? Two months ago, Alex had said. What had Howard been doing in that time? Then anger dominated her misery. He should have told her; she had a right to know what he was up to.

Bitterness got her through the rest of the day. She channelled it into her work. By eight o'clock her and Alex's desks were clear.

'The perfect secretary,' Alexander Drayton murmured as he switched on the answerphone for the night. 'I'll pick you up at ten.'

Carrie's eyes fluttered shut for a second. Slave driver! Hadn't she done enough for one day?

He read her. 'Dinner, not work.'

Her eyes widened as he brushed past and left the office.

Had she any choice? she asked herself, clipping gold rings to her ears later that evening; he hadn't waited for a reply, had taken it for granted she wouldn't object. She didn't; she wanted to go. Not because she sought Alex's company but because she was still so flaming mad with Howard that she didn't fancy her own company this night. She felt hopelessly lost. Where was he and how could she find him? And why, oh, why, hadn't he told her?

She wore red because that was the mood she was in. Fiery, though the style of the dress was skimpy and cool. Alex wore Italian grey, a lightweight suit that emphasised his dark Mediterranean colouring and the power of his physique.

The restaurant he drove her to was around the headland, several kilometres away from the marina, high up in the hills with breathtaking views down

to a moonlit bay surrounded by a mass of white
and silver: white-washed dwellings illuminated by
sparkling street lights. Carrie wasn't in the mood
to fully appreciate the beauty of it all. Instead she
wondered if Howard was in one of those villas. He
had rented close to the Puerto, now the Marina, of
course. Was he still here?

They sat on the terrace of the Swiss restaurant
and sipped Camparis till Carrie felt that tight coil
inside her begin to unwind.

'I've pushed you too hard today,' Alex said
softly. 'You look strained.'

'I'm used to that sort of pressure.'

'Not in this heat, though.'

'I can take it.' She smiled then because she felt
like it. Alex smiled back and she relaxed more. She
was over-reacting to Howard's not keeping her informed, she convinced herself. There was probably
a very simple answer to all this but for the moment
she wasn't prepared to think about it.

The wine Alex ordered for them, a smooth red
Rioja to accompany the steaks, faded Howard to
the back of her mind. They ate and drank and
talked about the Marina till Carrie found she was
enjoying herself.

'You wear an engagement ring.' It was the first
personal exchange between them.

Carrie looked down to the cluster of tiny sapph-
ires as if seeing them for the very first time. She
was tempted to lie about the ring, deny she was
engaged, claim the ring was her mother's and only
fitted that finger. But she didn't. She said nothing.

'So you will be marrying soon and you'll start a
family and leave.'

Carrie looked up at him. At the moment, she was so raw with anger over Howard that the thought palled.

'Do you object to your secretary being a married woman?' she hedged.

'I prefer it,' he told her, replenishing her empty glass.

'Safer?' Carrie queried, recalling his stormy relationship with Adela Carmen Rivera.

'Exactly,' he returned.

It occurred to her that she didn't know his marital status. He could be having an affair with his lawyer and have a wife too. She asked, 'Are you married?'

'No, but I came close once.'

'What stopped you?'

'Rumblings on the Stock Exchange.'

Carrie raised a quizzical brow, and he rose to it.

'I had to choose between losing a fortune or losing a love.' He gave her just enough to whet her appetite.

Leaning forward, Carrie, wide-eyed, husked, 'You went for the money?'

He shrugged his broad shoulders. 'A Stock Exchange crash. I locked myself in my City office for a month; when I came out I'd saved my fortune but lost the woman I was going to marry.' He raised his wine to his lips. Carrie's heart ached for him— only for a second though. What he said next shattered any pity she might have felt for him.

'It was the most exhilarating month of my life,' he stated quietly. 'Far more exhilarating than marriage to Fiona would have been.'

'How could you be sure if you didn't marry her?' Carrie asked bitingly.

'Because she married my widowed father.'

Stunned by that, Carrie nearly choked on her wine. She swallowed hard. 'Oh... I'm sorry...'

'Don't be,' he smiled, touched by her concern. 'She's happy spending his money in every capital of the world and he has a beautiful wife, young enough to be his daughter. It suits them both. I think I had a narrow escape, don't you?'

'Put like that, yes, I suppose you did.' She raised limpid eyes to his. 'But you couldn't have known that at the time, I mean you could have opted for her and not the money.'

'But I didn't, did I?'

'Which means you put a greater value on money than personal relationships?' she persisted.

He didn't answer her directly but said enough to confirm her thoughts. 'Money is a powerful aphrodisiac. It arouses and deeply satisfies.' He held her gaze over the candlelight in the centre of the table. 'It's comparable with making love to a beautiful woman, but in the long run much safer,' he added throatily.

That feeling of emptiness swamped her again. It was as if the rest of the crowded restaurant faded into a pink mist around them. She read his eyes. Man and woman. Not man and secretary. She sensed he might be testing her again, seeing how far she would go and not in a business context either! He was into affairs, not lasting relationships... No more drink, she vowed, pushing her glass away. She was imagining things. Alexander Drayton had more sense than to seek a flirtation with this secretary!

She definitely didn't imagine she had seen Adela Carmen Rivera, though. No mistaking the haunting beauty that turned the heads of all in the restaurant, but she hadn't turned Alex's head. He was sitting with his back to her. Carrie wondered what would happen if he turned and saw her dining with another man.

Adela and her escort, on the far side of the dining-room, had finished their meal and were preparing to leave when Adela caught sight of Carrie and Alex and tugged at the sleeve of her companion. It was in that second Carrie realised the folly of what she was doing here. She was dining with her boss; nothing so unusual in that but her boss and that woman were lovers and to get to be lovers they had probably started out this way. And who knew what was going through Adela's mind at this moment!

So what was she doing out with another man herself? Carrie couldn't see the man's face; he was turned away from her but ...

It was like a blow to the kidneys. An instant of recognition followed by a hot rush of inquisition. Why? How?

Suddenly he was upon them. Adela had disappeared like a phantom.

'Alex, how are you?'

'Howard. Good to see you back. How was Tokyo?' Alex half rose, and signalled to the waiter for another chair. 'Join us for coffee and a brandy. This is my new secretary, Carrie Sutherland. Carrie, my marketing manager, Howard Benson.'

Carrie didn't know whether to laugh, cry or scream. Her feminine intuition told her to keep quiet. It wasn't wrong.

She was out of context, she told herself. Not expecting to see her here in Spain *and* with his boss, how else could she expect him to react? Not like this! Her head spun as he held out a hand, and his eyes looked through her as if she didn't exist, as if he had never seen her before in his life!

'Pleased to meet you, Carrie.' His smile was a stranger's, his touch cool. 'Excuse me if I don't join you, Alex.' He looked at his watch, the watch Carrie had bought him for his thirtieth birthday! 'I'm expecting a call from Japan.'

'Is it looking good?' Alex asked, dark brows raised expectantly.

'Very. I'll bring you up to date in the morning.' Wishing them both good night, he left.

How Carrie got through the coffee and brandy stage she never knew. The brandy scoured her throat, and conversation died on her lips; anything Alex said went through the gap where her brain had once ticked. She felt empty, brain-dead!

They drove back to the Marina in silence, Carrie too stunned and confused to speak, Alex obviously regretting asking her out to dinner. When they reached the apartments Alex escorted her to her door, hoped she slept well and walked away down the marble-floored corridor, his hands deep in his trouser pockets.

The evening had been a disaster. She had bored Alexander Drayton nearly to death! And as for Howard...

Carrie kicked off her shoes, went to the kitchen and poured a glass of bottled water. Sliding back the patio doors, she stepped out on to the terrace to drink it. The fizzy water brought bubbles of questions and unsatisfactory answers to the surface of her mind. What was Howard playing at? How come he was working for Alex? And had he suffered some accident, a blow to his head that had wiped out her existence!

'Carrie! Carrie!' a rasping whisper caught her unawares and she jumped nervously. She looked over the balcony, clasped a hand to her skidding heart.

'Howard! What are you doing here?' she cried.

He silenced her with fingers on his lips, motioned to the apartment above hers and then beckoned her down to the gardens below.

She was there in seconds, expecting an apology, an explanation. Instead he grasped her wrist and fled with her, down cool passageways, far away from the apartments, into a small square, Carrie running to keep up with him, barefoot. The square was grassed, springy and cool underfoot. Howard pulled her down to a bench seat below an olive tree, tried to take her in his arms.

'Steady on,' she gasped, struggling for breath and pushing him away. 'What's going on, Howard? What on earth are you playing at?'

'Me? That's rich!' he spluttered and Carrie's heart sank. He hadn't changed. 'I couldn't believe my eyes when I saw you dining with Alex Drayton. What are *you* playing at, more to the point?'

Briefly Carrie explained about Tenson's. 'So when this job came up I jumped at it——'

'So you came down here to spy on me, eh?' he grated accusingly. 'Didn't trust me——'

'Cool it, Howard!' Carrie snapped. 'I want explanations, not a row. I want to know why you looked through me tonight in the restaurant. I want to know why you didn't tell me you were working for Marina del Oro——'

'OK! OK!' he rasped. 'How did you expect me to react when I saw you dining with my boss? I was in shock, I can tell you.'

'Funny way to act, if you ask me,' Carrie retorted. 'We are supposed to be engaged——'

'God! He doesn't know, does he? You didn't tell him you knew me?' He leapt up from the seat, and started to pace up and down.

'No, I didn't tell him I knew you,' Carrie said quietly. She'd been in a state of shock herself. 'But why the secrecy?'

He stopped pacing, and faced her. 'I wish you hadn't come, Carrie. You could mess up my whole career, do you realise that? You'd better go back to England——'

'Like hell I will!' she interrupted indignantly. 'You want me to jettison my career for yours? Give me one good reason.'

'Because this job is the best thing that has happened to me in years. You know what a rough time I've had. I don't want you here making waves for me.'

On a screech of exasperation, Carrie protested, 'And how am I supposed to make these waves, Howard?'

He didn't answer, but resumed pacing till Carrie wanted to scream with frustration. 'Howard,' she said at last. She'd forced calmness upon herself, determined to find out what was happening. 'I want to know exactly what is going on. I've never seen you so uptight. You're like a stranger to me. Since I've arrived I've found that Puerto del Sol is now the Marina del Oro, you are working for Alex, you've just come back from Tokyo...I didn't know any of this. Don't you think you owe me an explanation?'

He let out a ragged sigh and flopped down on the bench next to her. 'I didn't want to worry you, Carrie,' he murmured, not very convincingly to Carrie's ears. 'What do you know about the Puerto del Sol company?'

She shrugged. 'Only what Alex told me, that it was badly run and when he came in he changed the staff and renamed it. I had no idea you were still working here.'

'I wasn't for a while. Someone tipped me off that the crash was coming and I got out. Drayton moved in with his money, threw out all the original staff and reformed. I applied for the job of marketing manager, got it, and that's the story so far.'

'With a few chapters missing,' Carrie snorted. 'Why did you leave before the crash? You weren't to know he'd get rid of the staff.'

He rubbed his forehead. 'It was inevitable that he would. The Puerto del Sol company wasn't squeaky clean, Carrie,' he said resignedly.

So she and the media hadn't been wrong about time-share. She didn't say I told you so, though. Howard looked and sounded as if he'd found that out for himself, the hard way.

'When Drayton moved in it was the proverbial new brush sweeping clean. He didn't trust anyone, right down to the gardeners—everyone went. I wouldn't have stood a chance at this job if he suspected I'd worked for the original company. Look, darling...' he manoeuvred his arm around her shoulder '...I'm sorry if I upset you tonight. I've had a really tough time in Tokyo and it was such a shock seeing you. I was terrified that you would say something to Drayton. This job means a lot to me.'

Carrie understood, or at least thought she did. 'What were you doing out with Adela Carmen Rivera tonight?' *That* she couldn't understand.

'Business, sweetheart,' he laughed. 'I've been trying to tie up this Tokyo deal and there were some legal points I wanted to go over with Adela.'

'Couldn't it have waited till business hours?' She gave him a sidelong glance, and wasn't surprised to see defence sprint across his face. She was getting the strong impression that Howard and Adela were somehow romantically involved.

'Hey, come on! I didn't come over green when I saw you with Drayton, did I?'

He had a point but Carrie didn't want to dwell on it. 'A pity you didn't, Howard. It would have showed you cared!'

'That's not fair, Carrie,' he bleated.

'Life's not fair to you, is it, Howard?' She'd heard enough. She stood up to walk away but he grasped at her wrist and pulled her back.

'Carrie, sweetheart, I do care. You must know that.' He tried unsuccessfully to draw her into his arms.

'No, Howard.' She pushed him away. 'I don't want you to touch me. I need time to sort out my feelings.'

'You have doubts about our engagement, don't you?' he snapped, his tone implying that the fault lay with her.

'Don't you?'

He didn't answer for a while and that was answer enough. 'I do love you, Carrie,' he said at last.

'But not enough,' she told him icily. 'If you did, you would have been honest with me, told me all about the Puerto del Sol, confided in me. We can't have a relationship if there is no trust, Howard.'

'I've made mistakes, Carrie, I admit that. But I don't want it to end like this.'

'Five minutes ago you wanted me to go back to England, were terrified I was going to jeopardise your job for you.'

'I still think you should go back. We've more chance of working things out if we are apart than if we try working together,' he bit out.

Carrie's eyes widened in surprise. 'I fail to see how you work that one out.'

He stood up. 'If you stay you'll soon find out what I mean. It's not easy working for Drayton, you need your wits about you. He'll draw the last drop of blood from you to get what he wants.'

'So if you're under that sort of pressure why do you stay?'

Plunging his hands deep into his trouser pockets he laughed wryly. 'With my track record, darling, I'm the kiss of death to any company. Not this one, though. I might not like Drayton very much but I know a winner when I see one. Mr Alexander Drayton is going to make me a lot of money.'

'Well, I'd say you're both tarred with the same brush. I'm sure you'll go a long way with each other,' Carrie clipped.

'I've no doubt about that,' Howard muttered. He looked down at her. 'I still want you to share in my success, Carrie. Let's not be hasty. Let's see how things go. When you get back to England you may be able to see things more clearly.'

She gave him a wry smile. 'That was precisely the reason I came here in the first place, to see things more clearly.'

'What do you mean?' Howard frowned.

'It doesn't matter, Howard, it doesn't matter any more.' She sighed wearily and looked up at him. 'I'm staying on with the company. I'm only here for a couple of months so I won't cramp your style with Adela.'

He shook his head vigorously. 'Come on now, Carrie. There is nothing going on there. She's Drayton's lady, not mine!'

Was that why she had fled from the restaurant? Was she two-timing Alexander Drayton? The thought was amusing but not one she wished to dwell on. Suddenly she was too tired to think.

'I'm sorry, Carrie. I still think we have a chance. Maybe it will all work out.'

Carrie shook her head, knowing there wasn't a chance in hell. How could there be? It had been bad enough in England—now she had come out here and found that Howard was living a life that she wasn't even considered in.

'Carrie, I don't see any reason to let on we knew each other before,' he said. 'And I trust you not to mention anything to Drayton about my working for Puerto del Sol. Let sleeping dogs lie in that direction, eh?

'I'd better go now. Don't want to run the risk of being seen together, do we?' He kissed her lightly on the tip of her nose and disappeared into the darkness.

Carrie slumped down on the bench seat when he had gone, held her head in her hands. So that was it, was it? The end of her engagement. However had it come about in the first place? Somehow they had drifted into it; all their friends were doing likewise, it had seemed inevitable that Carrie and Howard would follow suit. But where had love come in all this? She had loved him, once, but that seemed like aeons ago. So much had happened since. Howard had changed when he had lost his job but thousands of other people lost their jobs and it didn't break up their relationships. Theirs obviously hadn't been solid enough.

It all served as a warning to her, though. Marriage was a serious business, not to be entered into lightly. Dismal though the thought was, like Alexander Drayton she'd had a narrow escape.

At last she stood up, started back to the apartment, so tired she could hardly keep her eyes open. Silently she cursed Howard for not escorting her back to the apartment. She hadn't a clue where she was going.

Carrie stopped suddenly. This was the wrong way. She didn't remember this clump of yuccas. One lashed her arm and she rubbed the graze fretfully.

Hot and irritated with herself, she turned back only to panic as she nearly toppled down a flight of steep stone steps that hadn't been there before. Of course they'd been there, she reasoned, running down them and swinging to the left. She stopped. Dead end. She twisted round, eyes searching menacing black tunnels that by day had been bright, pretty walkways.

She was lost, hopelessly lost in a maze of stone walls and harsh pathways under her bare feet. Damn Howard. He knew the layout better than she did. Anger with him flared.

A trickle of moisture ran down the small of her back as she suddenly froze in terror. Her silky dress clung to the *frissons* of fear that electrified her body. There was someone nearby, a foot on the clay tiles behind her. Carrie ran, ran for her life.

A scream jarred in her throat as she rounded another corner. A hand reached out and grabbed her wrist, spun her back and into a wall of heated muscle. Two powerful arms encircled her, pressed her body close to his.

She knew the smell, sensed the safety, sobbed out his name.

'Alex!'

If she thought she was safe she was wrong. Hot lips scored hers in a fury of passion. The whole desperate night rushed in on her and she clung to him, her breasts heaving with exertion, her heart bursting, her mouth burning with a need.

'Dear God!' he rasped at last, his voice raw and harsh deep in his throat. 'If you must tear barefoot through the night like a wild gypsy you'll have to suffer the consequences.' His mouth came to hers again, brutally, out of control. Carrie couldn't fight it—horrified, she realised she didn't want to. Her lips parted with a gasp and her fingers splayed out in his hair. She was so hot that her body was wet, her dress damp and moulded to her skin, her hair moist and plastered to her flaming cheeks. The fire that burned inside her ate up any resistance, weakened every moral fibre of her soul.

Drunk with a need she didn't understand, she let him crush her to the intimate hardness of him, let his mouth caress her naked breast. Had she helped him slip down the shoulder straps of her dress? She didn't know and didn't care; the heat of his passion and her own arousal cast modesty to the night sky. She moaned as his mouth came back to hers scented with her own perfume, and then it happened. The floodtides crashed through the barrier of her subconcious and with a sob she cried. Hot tears of anger, frustration and more... More than anything she cried for something she didn't understand, this burning need for this man who had grasped her fear in his arms and taken such brutal advantage of her momentary weakness.

'You shouldn't have done that,' she sobbed.

'You shouldn't look like that at this time of night,' he growled, holding her shuddering body away from him. 'What are you up to, Carrie?'

He was angry and Carrie wasn't naïve enough not to know why. His voice, raw and ravaged, betrayed his sheer frustration. Her body still seared with the aftermath of his passionate assault, the assault she had needed, encouraged, the assault she had hysterically halted with the impact of ice on fire.

'I . . . I went for a walk. Co . . . couldn't find my way back. I thought I heard someone. I was so afraid.' She raised her tear-filled eyes to his, the realisation of just what had happened draining the blood from her lips. Slowly, eyes wide with horror, she lifted the thin strap of her dress over her shoulder. Alex manoeuvred the other for her, his fingers crazing a trail of fire on her moist flesh. She shivered uncontrollably. He felt it.

'Cold or shocked?' His voice had returned to near normal.

'Shocked,' she whispered. In that instant of impact against his body she had known desire on a scale that Howard's caresses had never registered on. She was afraid of that desire now, ashamed of it because he had registered that need.

'Shocked that we nearly went too far. Nearly made love here in this walkway?'

In horror Carrie fell away from him—voiced so openly it sounded worse. Weakly she slumped back against a rough white wall. It was cool and sobering and Carrie spread her fingers against the coarseness of it. 'We didn't and it wouldn't have happened.'

'It could have done so very easily, Carrie, and that mystifies me.'

'Wh . . . what do you mean?' She was still breathless she realised, still slightly panicky, her breasts heaving under the red silk.

'You're engaged to be married, remember?' he said softly. 'Strange behaviour for someone in love with another man. Or was that the problem? Were you thinking of him, wanting him? Did your frustration drive you out into the night to seek appeasement? If you hadn't hammered into me, would anyone have done?

'You bastard!' she breathed heavily, nausea rising in her stomach at the thought. 'How could you...?' She turned blindly away.

Somehow she found the apartment, her inner radar guiding her just when she needed it most. She slammed the heavy door, twisted the key viciously in the lock.

She stripped, showered, lay in bed stiff with tension. No more tears; they wouldn't come. Her world hung in shreds. Tonight she had coldly and callously ended her engagement to a man who had deceived her and minutes later let a man she hardly knew, barely liked, nearly make love to her. And Alexander Drayton of all people, the man who signed her pay cheques!

Wild gypsy, he had called her, and that was how he had made her feel, that was what he had aroused in her: passion, fire and a savage sexuality she hadn't realised she possessed.

Hours into the night she was still wrestling with strange emotions coursing through her veins, so restless she wanted to scream. What sort of woman was she who could let a man do that, touch her body in such a way, ravage her lips so cruelly?

She tried to think of Howard, Howard who had never... She sat up in bed, covered her face with her hands. Howard had never shown such raw passion. Was that another reason her love for him had withered away? Did she have a need deep inside her, one she had not recognised till tonight?

She lay back on the pillows, exhausted. No, she wasn't that sort of girl. She should have tried harder with Howard, fought to save her future with him. Her mind twisted crazily and as she finally slipped into a troubled sleep her last miserable thought was that it was Alexander Drayton's mouth that featured primarily in her tortured thinking.

CHAPTER THREE

'TAKE the white Escort from the car pool at the back of administration.' Alex Drayton tossed a bunch of keys on to Carrie's desk. 'You'll need your own transport. One of the girls will advise you about the best place to shop. I believe there is a hypermarket further along the coast.' He went into his office and closed the door behind him.

Drayton by day, Dracula by night! She had been dreading facing him, half expected a dismissal to be on the agenda this morning. By not referring to last night's fracas in the scented walkway he'd made it easier for her. If he could forget it so could she. It had been a case of being in the wrong place at the wrong time, as rare as birds colliding in flight. It wouldn't happen again.

Ten minutes later Howard walked into her office. 'Good morning, Carrie. It is Carrie, isn't it? Is Alex free?'

Carrie gave him a murderous look which he returned with a supercilious grin. Was she going mad? Had last night ever happened?

After checking that Alex was prepared to see him—she was a quick learner—she showed him into the inner sanctum.

'Coffee in ten minutes please, Carrie,' Alex told her as she closed the door.

Carrie delegated that task. Domestic duties had not been expected of her in the past and she saw no reason to veer from that now. Though she did condescend to take the tray in when it arrived. Alex and Howard were poring over sales figures, impervious to her and the coffee she was pouring.

'What are you doing?' Two hours later, an hour after Howard had left without acknowledging her at her desk, Alex emerged from his office. He came and stood behind her. 'Is all that necessary?' He peered over her shoulder at the rippling screen of the computer.

'Your files are in a mess. They need sorting out. I like to do things my own way.'

'Which means you are staying,' he grated in her left ear.

She wouldn't turn round. 'I suppose you expected me to resign after last night,' she stated flatly, shifting files into memory while she juggled space on the disk. 'I'm not a silly little teenager and I'm not a wild gypsy, no matter what you think.'

He spun her swivel chair till she faced him, steadied the back with one hand, the other splayed out on the desk. His breath was warm, a sensual reminder of last night.

'Ice by day, fire by night. You're an enigma, do you know that?'

Carrie almost laughed at the similar metaphor she had found for him. His mouth was so dangerously close that she could almost feel its soft caress. Were those lips capable of a soft caress? What she knew of them so far was otherwise. Brutal, demanding, insatiable.

'You're turning me into an enigma,' she told him softly. 'You misinterpreted what happened last night. I was so frightened I just fell into your arms. A situation like that was a one-off.'

'Are you tempting me to prove that it wasn't? he said gravely. 'Because if you are, forget those sort of games. I don't play.'

'Well, get out of the playground!' Carrie retorted and tried to swivel back to the screen. He was having none of that. He held on.

'If we're not playing games, where's the ring this morning?'

'It . . . it slipped off in the shower last night,' she lied. She could hardly tell him the truth, that she'd broken off her engagement to his marketing manager and the ring was where her future with Howard was, in the past.

'A Freudian slip, no doubt,' he mocked sarcastically, spun her back to the computer and went back to his office, closing the door so softly behind him that it jarred more than if he had slammed it.

Right from the start she had known it wouldn't be easy to work for him. Sir Michael would have been appalled if he could have heard the last few minutes' rejoinders. He had been such a gentleman to work for. A traditionalist in every way. As an employer Alexander Drayton broke rules, made his own. Well, he should expect repercussions. He hadn't wanted a yes woman and he hadn't got one. She could give as much as she could take but from now on she would avoid close encounters of a sensual kind.

'No siesta this afternoon, Carrie,' he told her at two. 'We're going to look at the golf course.'

'What golf course?' she asked, gathering her straw bag up and following him down the corridor.

'I didn't know we had one.' She hadn't seen anything remotely resembling a course on the plans.

'We haven't as yet but we're going to have to arrange one pretty quickly. The Japanese are golf crazy.'

There was no chance for further questioning as Alex held the passenger door open for her. She slid in, adjusted her denim blue cotton skirt, swung round in surprise as someone got into the back of the car.

'Is Enrique meeting us on site?' Alex asked as he started the engine.

'Enrique and John Summers. Enrique managed to track him down in Marbella, on the green of course. He sent the chopper down for him.'

She knew that voice. Carrie sat stiffly, staring into space ahead of her. It was unbearable, sitting next to Alex with Howard in the back discussing business so calmly. They would never be able to keep this up, this pretence of not knowing each other.

They drove up beyond the foundation work of the complex that was well in progress, crossed a dual carriageway and drove higher into the hills, the narrow dirt road twisting in and out of forests of cypresses heady with pine scent. Carrie was surprised it was so green and fertile up here, for beyond this part of the foothills the Sierras rose majestically, grey and hazy blue, wind-dried and savage.

They stopped when the road petered out to a footpath. Almost immediately a Land Rover pulled up behind them. Two men got out and the smaller of the two introduced John Summers, a huge American, complete with B-movie accent, birds of paradise shirt and a token chunk of cigar jutting from his mouth.

Carrie could hardly contain her amusement.

'I agree, larger than life, isn't he?' Alex said as he dropped into step beside her. The others had gone ahead, the track winding up through the pines, only wide enough to take two. 'He's designed some of the most prestigious golf courses in the world. Lives for golf.'

Carrie smiled and shook her head. 'It always amazes me what grown men see in whacking a little ball into a hole in the ground.'

'Heaven forbid!' Alex ground out. 'Don't let the jolly green giant hear a statement like that. He looks the sort to murder for less.'

She glanced at him, wondered if her opinion was out of line. He was smiling, a heart-lurching smile of near perfect white teeth, teeth that had ground against hers ... She looked away quickly, pointed out a lizard on the path and felt childish for doing so.

'One day, Carrie, I'll take you round a course, teach you the art and the delight of caressing a wood and guiding that precious sphere to its goal.'

Carrie's breath caught in her throat. Had he meant to make that statement sound so suggestive? She was so shocked at it that she stumbled, quickly regained her balance and heard soft laughter from deep in his throat. He had.

He walked ahead of her, leaving her with her blushes.

'I'd say you've bought yourself a chunk of heaven up here Alex,' John Summers bellowed from a clearing. 'There's water underground, I can smell it. It'll be simple to irrigate. We'll sink a few bore holes, tap the natural resources to keep the conservationists happy.' He laughed out loud at that and Carrie grimaced. 'We'll hack the top off this hill here, it'll be as easy as slicing the top off a boiled egg . . .'

Carrie didn't want to hear any more. She wandered away, slumped down on to a fallen pine, eased her hot feet out of her sandals.

'I don't believe this. Are they really planning a golf course up here?' she whispered to Howard who was standing back from the others. 'Howard, I'm speaking to you!'

'Well, don't, Carrie,' was all he said and tightlipped at that. He strolled away and joined Enrique who was hanging on every word John Summers bellowed. Carrie fumed to herself.

Alex beckoned her over and, taking a pad and pen from her bag, she joined them.

Alex wanted a record of all that was being discussed and Carrie worked furiously, glad to have her mind occupied other than raging over Howard.

Later, as they walked back to the cars, Carrie found herself walking with Alex again.

'I suppose you are all absolutely serious about this; it's not some joke at my expense, is it? There is going to be a golf course here one day?' She gazed around her at the rocky terrain. There were varying degrees of small valleys and gullies and the hilltop Summers was all for slicing like the top of a boiled egg was a small mountain really.

'Can't your imagination run to visualising greens, bunkers and fairways here?'

'I'm afraid it can't,' Carrie replied frostily. 'And to be frank the very idea appals me. It will spoil the natural beauty of the place.'

He laughed then. 'I suppose I asked for this, you giving opinions. Go on, then, you'd better make it good.'

Carrie stopped. 'Why, it won't make an iota of difference. You'll do it whatever I say.'

He faced her, tall and daunting, the pine-scented breeze lifting wisps of black hair from his forehead.

'You're right, it won't make any difference to the project but it will make a difference to me. I'm curious for your thoughts.' He plunged his hands into the pockets of his off-white linen trousers, and rocked back on his heels. 'Come on,' he teased. 'Let's hear it for the ecologists.'

Biting her lower lip hard, Carrie turned away. Ruthless. A perfect description for this man. He'd slice through mountains to make a buck.

'Carrie.'

She turned and faced him with that defiant tilt of her chin. He leaned back against a tree, his powerful arms folded across his chest.

'Come back here, Carrie,' he said, so compellingly that she went. She stood before him. He lifted a lazy hand to tuck a strand of hair behind her ear. The effect was catastrophic on her senses. Nothing around her seemed real any more.

'I'm sorry if I sounded insincere but I know exactly what is going through your mind. You're wrong, you know.'

She looked beyond him, over his shoulder, down the pine-tree-covered hillside to where the marina lay tranquil in the palm of a turquoise bay.

'Wrong to want to conserve that?' She nodded at the glorious views beyond him.

He deigned to move his head and flick his eyes over the vista. 'That will still be there when the course is down,' he said quietly, turning his head back to gauge her reaction.

'This won't be, though.' She waved her hand at the beautiful landscape immediately around them, the trees, yellow gorse and wild rosemary.

'True, but there will be something equally lovely in its place. Because something is new doesn't mean it can't be beautiful.'

'I know, but...' She wavered, seeing his point.

'But what?'

She tilted her head to one side, a ghost of a smile played on her lips. 'A golf course?'

He smiled back at her, his dark eyes soft in the filtered sun that dappled through the branches over their heads.

'"Green, I love you, green. Green wind. Green branches,"' he quoted softly.

Stunned, Carrie's heart pumped. *This* side of the man was potentially dangerous, probably more dangerous than the aggressive side of him. She lowered her eyes in confusion.

'I don't think the poet, Lorca, had the eighteenth hole in mind when he wrote that!' She said it deliberately sarcastically, to puncture the hazy balloon that was forming around them. She started to walk back, heard him crunching behind her on the shingle path.

'So you think it would be a mistake to create a golf course out of a dying pine forest?'

She looked to each side of the track. 'I see no evidence of that.'

Her hand was grasped suddenly and she was pulled from the track, down a small incline. Breathless, she stood next to him, every nerve in her body alert. He didn't release her hand, but held it as if it was the most natural thing in the world to do.

'I see plenty of evidence,' he said, pointing with his other hand to a copse to their left. Huge pines stood gaunt and barren, some already fallen. 'Nothing lives for ever, Carrie.'

Her eyes followed the line of his long fingers, hardly able to see clearly because of the heat haze around her. Why should she feel like this when he was so close? Burning inside. She was tempted to run away, through the trees, down to that glimmer of water beyond the copse. Run like a wild gypsy...

'Saplings could be planted,' she argued, her breath coming in a hot rush.

'They will be. And lakes created and wildlife preserved—— '

'And all so rich tourists can plonk balls into holes.' She scrambled back up the incline to the track, anxious to get away from him.

'Tourism in Spain provides one point three million jobs and earns in excess of sixteen billion dollars. One in nine Spaniards live well and raise families from tourism...'

This was Alexander Drayton the financier talking. She knew he was right, of course. Knew deep down that the course when completed would probably be an area of outstanding beauty. People these days were so much more caring of their en-

vironment. Politicians, industrialists, even international financiers like Drayton were thinking
green. So why had she put up the defences when
she knew whatever Alex was planning would be
ecologically acceptable? He might be ruthless but
he could quote Lorca...

That was it, she decided as they walked back to
the cars. The man was unfolding in front of her
and she didn't want to see the side that wasn't hard
and implacable. It was safer to have something to
despise. Already she was admitting to his attract-
iveness and that wasn't on. He had a lady, Adela,
and after Howard Carrie wasn't about to enter
another risky relationship. She would need to
remind herself of that if she was to survive.

Howard was leaning on the bonnet of Alex's car
when they emerged from the trees. At sight of them
Howard jerked away from the car, a small gesture
which irritated Carrie. The expression on his face
irritated her too. A scowl marred his usual golden
good looks.

'And what's wrong with you?' she asked as she
opened the passenger door and got in, leaving it
ajar so she could speak to him. Alex was well out
of earshot and fully occupied with Enrique and the
big American.

'You took long enough to get back here.
Drayton's not coming on to you, is he?' he hissed
between clenched teeth.

Carrie closed her eyes in momentary despair. 'No,
he's not,' she answered firmly. 'We were discussing
the new golf course, something you could have explained if you weren't so paranoid about associ-
ating with me.'

He didn't reply to that but broke into a trot when Alex raised a beckoning hand to him. Carrie could imagine him bleating, yes, sir, no, sir . . . She bit her lip. That thinking was unkind. Howard was doing his best.

She was later to hear that Howard's best was very much merited by Alexander Drayton. They stopped at the Marina del Oro pizzeria for lunch, Alex insisting.

The restaurant was cedar-built with a thatched roof and a secluded terrace overlooking the tennis courts. Each gingham-covered table was shaded by a raffia umbrella with long fringes that rustled softly in the breeze. They sat down and ordered pizzas and soft drinks.

'Howard is about to pull off the sales coup of the decade.' Alex started to explain. 'He's about to close a deal with a Japanese car company. They were interested in twenty units for investment and incentive marketing within their company and Howard has succeeded in pushing them to take forty.'

'And you're constructing the golf course for them as part of the deal? I wouldn't have thought that cost-effective,' she commented.

Both men looked united in their surprise at her remark.

'You're partly right, Carrie.' Alex spoke quietly, his sharp gaze assessing her in a new way. 'The profits on those forty units won't cover the cost of the course but it's a start, a damned good start. The rest is up to Howard and his team. They've broken into a very lucrative market in the Japanese and they love golf so we'll give them what they want. The prospects are enormous.'

Alex and Howard went on discussing those heady prospects as they ate, Carrie lapsing into silence. So the Japanese were scheduled to arrive later in the month, and Alex was scheduled to fly to Geneva soon after. Carrie, for the first time, wished she could go home.

After struggling with a pizza Napoletana she pushed her plate away and excused herself.

Leaving the two men, who showed no sign of breaking for a siesta, she strolled back to the administration centre and picked up a car from the company pool.

She found the hypermarket along the coast with no trouble and spent a pleasant half-hour familiarising herself with Spanish provisions. She shopped for one, a dismal thought she tried not to dwell on too deeply.

'Oh, no!' Carrie groaned. Sparks flew from the electric kettle as she switched it on. 'Damn!' was her lightning follow-up as the kitchen light snapped out.

She stood for a while, her eyes getting used to the darkness, then groped her way round the apartment checking the other lights. Nothing. She'd somehow managed to fuse the whole apartment. Or was it a general power failure?

The harbour lights were on but Carrie guessed those ran from a separate system. And none of the other apartments was occupied so she couldn't tell if they were out as well.

Alex? She hadn't seen him since the pizzeria. He had phoned the office at six to say he wouldn't be in that evening and left her to manage on her own, which suited her perfectly. Was he in his apartment?

Did she honestly need this bedtime cup of tea? she asked herself. She could survive without it but what about the morning? She couldn't start the day without a shot of caffeine and if she didn't blow-dry her hair first thing she would look like that wild gypsy...

Savagely she abandoned the thought of troubling Alex at this hour; what time was it? About eleven? She started to undress for bed, then stopped abruptly at the undies stage. Was she crazy? Supposing there was a fault in her electricity circuit? Supposing... why, it could be happening now, two wires touching, sparking, igniting! Panic surged her into a T-shirt and jeans.

He was in, relief swamped her as she rapped on the door. She could hear music.

She wasn't prepared for the impact on her senses as he swung open the door. He filled the doorway, tall, powerful, his hair ragged as if he'd been dragging his fingers through it. Cool cotton jeans hung low on his hips and his shirt flapped open exposing hard tanned muscle. Other senses clamoured for recognition, his cologne assailed her, spiced and heady, suiting his dark Mediterranean looks. The music she recognised as one of her favourite pieces, the intermezzo from *Cavalleria Rusticana*...

'I seem to be out, I mean my lights have gone...I plugged the kettle...and phut!' she gabbled.

He smiled and ushered her in. 'Catastrophe,' he murmured and Carrie wondered if he was being sarcastic. 'Make yourself comfortable while I rake around for a torch.'

He strode into the kitchen, leaving her to gaze around her in surprise. The apartment was exactly the same as hers. She hadn't expected that. Somehow she had presumed his apartment would be far superior. The furnishings were the same, the layout identical. The only variation on the theme was a console of telephones banked on the far wall of the sitting area and an elegant Bang and Olufsen sound system posing in the corner.

He'd been working, she noticed. Papers were scattered on the dining-table, some on the floor. The patio doors were wide open and a sudden gust of wind fluttered them dangerously and Carrie stepped forward to slide the doors shut. Her fingers whitened around the glass. The terrace table was set for two. Two fluted crystal wine glasses, one bottle of champagne on ice. He was expecting someone, and no prizes for guessing who.

'I'm sorry,' she said dismally, turning as he came back into the room. 'You're expecting someone. I didn't mean . . . look, the morning will do.' She was aware of a heightening of her colour, her temperature soaring.

'Adela won't be here for a while yet. I don't like the thought of you spending the night without electricity.' He had in his hand a powerful torch, an assortment of kitchen knives.

It was then that Carrie saw the futility of it all—she couldn't help but smile. 'Maybe it wasn't a good idea to ask for your help . . . perhaps in the morning maintenance can sort it out.' Her eyes never left the knives and suddenly Alexander Drayton laughed.

'Don't you think I'm capable of doing the job?'

'With kitchen knives?' She doubted if he knew what a screwdriver looked like.

'They will have to do; these apartments don't come supplied with do-it-yourself kits.'

'I should think not. Hardly inspires confidence in Spanish workmanship.'

He laughed at that and together they went down to her apartment.

'Where's the offending kettle?' he asked as he snapped on the torch.

Carrie led him to the kitchen, the darkness making her more intently aware of him. She stood away from him as he picked up the kettle.

'It's all right, it won't bite, you know,' he said quietly.

It wasn't the kettle she was afraid of! After a quick inspection he picked up the kettle and the lead and deposited them in the pedal bin.

'Lethal,' he said gravely. 'You didn't get a shock, did you?' He turned to her, his face deeply shadowed from the torch beam on the work surface.

'No... no. I switched it on from the plug on the wall. It just sparked.'

'You were lucky.' He picked up the torch, sounded angry. 'I think everyone associated with Puerto del Sol had some sort of fiddle going.'

Surprised, Carrie asked, 'What do you mean?'

'The place was corrupt. That was probably a job lot supplied by someone's cousin and invoiced at some exorbitant rate. Tomorrow I'll get maintenance to check every damned appliance on the marina.' He strode through the sitting-room and into the small entrance hall, taking with him the knives and the torch.

'What do you mean, the place was corrupt?' Carrie ventured to ask from the doorway. Howard had said that the company hadn't been quite above board.

'Misappropriation of company monies. It ran through every department like a virus. Sales were worse—so many angles being worked it was amazing they got away with it for so long.'

Poor Howard, he must have been sickened when he'd found out what was going on, and no wonder Alex had got rid of the old staff. He couldn't have trusted any of them.

'You'll have to hold this torch for me, Carrie.'

She hurried to his side, took the torch from his outstretched hand, and shone it on the junction box behind the front door.

'Watch what I'm doing because you might have to do this yourself one day.' He unscrewed the casing of the junction box with the tip of one of the knives, his long brown fingers working deftly. 'Hold out your hand.'

She held her free palm up and he dropped the loose screws into it. 'If there's a fault anywhere the electricity automatically cuts out. It's quite simple. See, all the switches are off; just flick them down and press this button to reset them.' He didn't do it but stepped back to let her get closer.

Already the screws had stuck to her palm. She tried to control the beam of the torch but it seemed to sway from side to side as her fingers trembled around it. Did he have to stand so close? The combined heat of their bodies in such a small space was making her dizzy. She desperately tried to dismiss last night from her mind, thought she had coped so well today. But she wasn't coping now—his nearness was causing her pulse to race, her heart to pump dangerously.

Without a word he took the torch from her so she had a free hand to manipulate the switches. He stood right behind her, directing the beam over her shoulder. His other hand came up to the back of her neck, his thumb caressed the small hollow under her hair. She didn't know what to say or do, so hypnotic was the caress, then a crazy thought spiralled through her mind—if she was electrocuted he would die too.

With tremulous fingers she thrust down the switches but then as she went for the reset button which would flood the apartment with light his hand closed over hers.

'Don't let's rush it now,' he said huskily, his voice so deep it reverberated through her. His mouth murmured against her hair and the heat of his body pressed against her back sent a shiver of despair through her. How easily he could alert every pulse in her body. She seemed to be on fire, crackling with searing heat that demanded fuelling. For seconds she couldn't move, so transfixed with all the incredible sensations powering through her that she was fused to the spot.

'Don't,' she whispered, hardly audible over the sound of his ragged breath. 'Don't' was not a word he recognised—his lips blazed down her neck, his arms tightened around her, pulling her back to meld into his own arousal.

A gasp caught in her throat, melted into a groan. He turned her to face him, and covered her mouth with his.

The torch clattered to their feet, throwing them into darkness, dangerous darkness. Inhibitions were lost in the dark, Carrie's whirling subconcious warned her. She took no heed, but wrapped her arms around his neck. He needed no more encouragement—his mouth took on a new raging assault, his hands moving over her body, drawing her deeper and deeper into him.

His mouth grazing over her breasts brought a small sob from deep within her. The sound drove him to draw hard on her nipples, draining her of any last resistance, drowning her in a need that was desperately painful. His hand went down to her jeans as his mouth seared back to hers, and he cupped her, grazed his fingers against the coarse denim between her thighs.

'Alex!' The call came like a death knell. 'Alex! Where the hell are you?'

Dazed, Carrie gasped. A sound like a muted roar came from Alex's throat. He didn't move away from her right away, but held on to her, knowing it couldn't end so cruelly and harshly. His mouth this time was different—because it was to be unfulfilled it took on a resigned softness, a poignancy that tore through Carrie's heart.

He moved away from her then, out of the small hallway through the sitting-room to the terrace. It was then that Carrie realised that Adela's call had come from his balcony.

'I'll be back in a minute,' he called up, giving no explanation of why he was on his secretary's terrace.

He came back to Carrie and pressed the reset button of the junction box over her shoulder.

Carrie was grateful that they were not flooded in cold harsh light. The hallway was still deep in shadow—the only light came from a lamp in the sitting-room which she had left on, but nevertheless she closed her eyes for an instant. When she opened them he was towering in front of her, his palm held up.

She opened hers. The screws had ground into the soft skin of her palm. Alex picked them out, lifted her hand and tenderly kissed the small indentations.

He replaced the screws without a word and gathered up the torch and the assortment of knives.

'To be continued,' he murmured, and reached out for the door-knob.

What possessed her she never knew, but she stopped him with her hand on his arm.

'No, Alex,' she said firmly, her eyes wide and bright with unshed tears. 'We can't.' She let out a deep shuddering sigh. 'I work for you. I like the work. I don't——'

'Want to lose my job,' he finished for her.

She couldn't tell him there was much much more to it than that. She was in danger of losing her heart as well.

'I'm not promiscuous,' she murmured. 'I'm not one of those women who could just have an affair.'

'And of course we mustn't forget the fiancé, must we?' He sounded angry.

Carrie blinked her lashes nervously. Not for one second when Alex had been making love to her had she thought of Howard and if he hadn't spoken of him then she knew it wouldn't have come into her reasoning later.

'Yes,' she uttered resignedly, 'we mustn't forget my fiancé.'

He smiled then, not with pleasure. 'I'd like to meet this man one day. See exactly what sort of a fool he is.'

'Fool?' Carrie breathed quickly.

He reached out with his free hand, took her by the back of her neck and pulled her against him. His mouth was hard and hot on hers, a kiss that punished. When he released her he grated, 'If you were my woman I'd keep you under lock and key, for my own sweet pleasure,' he added with harsh finality.

CHAPTER FOUR

CARRIE had it all figured out by the end of the week. She'd leave, of course. Not immediately, though she had every reason to. No, she would work till this term in Spain was over and then she would resign. Return to England and go back on the agency books.

She'd heard of sexual harassment at work before. A friend had lost a very good position because of unwanted advances by her middle-aged, my-wife-doesn't-understand-me boss.

But Alex wasn't middle-aged and he didn't have a wife to misunderstand him and his advances hadn't been altogether unwanted, though it was hard to admit to that. He was attractive and had his moments of humour and concern and she was beginning to like him more than she cared too.

So where did the sexual harassment come in? What a horrid expression anyway. Twice he had kissed her; more than that, he had come very close to making love to her all the way. So what?

She clung to the edge of his desk, which she was tidying, and closed her eyes as fantasies swamped her. Not for her an office romance, a few snatched hours after the rest of the staff had gone home. And that was how it would be with Alexander Drayton; it couldn't be anything else.

'Alone at last!' Someone came up behind her and squeezed her tightly round the waist.

'Howard! Don't be ridiculous! Alex could walk in any moment.'

'Not unless he's Superman. He's in Granada. I've just spoken to him on the phone.'

She'd known where he was but her excuse had been instinctive. 'And because he's miles away you feel free to manhandle me, do you?' She twisted away from him and carried on tidying the desk.

'Come on, Carrie, that's not fair.' He sounded hurt and though Carrie didn't look at him she guessed that lower lip of his would be pouting like a small boy's.

'Don't start that again, Howard.' She hadn't seen him since the pizzeria lunch. He had been avoiding her, she knew. She wondered what he wanted now. She bent down and locked the drawers of the desk. 'Did you want something?'

'You, as it happens.'

She straightened up, nerve-ends on alert.

'Don't look so panic-stricken, sweetheart. I'm not proposing anything immoral or illegal. I just happen to have an evening spare and would like to take you out for old times' sake.'

Carrie just had to laugh. 'You really know how to make a girl feel wanted, don't you?'

Howard missed her sarcasm.

'So what had you got in mind?' she asked. She had a spare evening too. Come to think of it, every evening was spare!

'A delightful Spanish restaurant in the hills, dancing on the terrace, a quiet moonlight drive back?'

A few months ago it would have sounded just perfect. Now the thought dismayed her.

'Pass,' she clipped.

'I wasn't making a pass at you, as it happens——'

'I didn't mean that...' She looked at him and felt a pang of sadness.

'Come on Carrie, let's go out and have a break. It will do us both good to get away from the Marina.'

All work and no pleasure was beginning to drag her down. A night out would perk her up.

'Why not?' she shrugged.

He stepped towards her and instinctively she took a step back. 'Howard, just friends, remember,' she warned, dark eyes narrowing.

He feigned a hurt expression then grinned widely. 'OK, you win. You can't blame a guy for trying.'

The first doubt surfaced. Maybe this wasn't such a good idea after all. If he thought he could win her back with dinner and soft music he was mistaken.

The second doubt came when he arranged to pick her up behind the complex, not at her apartment, claiming not to want to run the risk of their being seen together by Alex. So what was wrong with two of his employees going out together? For all he knew they had just struck up a friendship; he didn't need to know they had once been engaged and, as for divulging that he had worked for Puerto del Sol, she was the last person to blow the job for him, being the only one out here who knew just how important it was to him.

It was as they were dancing together, on the moonlit terrace of that little Spanish restaurant in the hills, that she realised what a fool she was to let things go this far.

'Relax, darling,' he breathed in her ear.

'How can I, Howard? You said just friends and you are holding me far too tightly.' She prised him away from her and stormed back to their table.

'Other couples are having a good time. I don't see why you can't just relax and enjoy yourself,' Howard breathed petulantly.

'Because it's different now,' she insisted, glowering at him across the candlelit table. 'And you are pawing me, Howard, and I don't like it.'

'You never objected before,' he iced at her, his blue eyes dark with annoyance. He poured himself another glass of wine and gulped it down.

'We were engaged before and every-thing . . . everything is different now,' she repeated dismally. She looked away from him, concentrated on the other dancers swaying romantically to soft, rhythmic guitars.

So very different, she reflected. And Alex Drayton had a lot to do with the sudden revulsion she felt at the cloying closeness of Howard. He'd spoiled her for ever more. She didn't understand that, for the life of her she couldn't see how he had changed her so drastically. All she knew was that if he were here, holding her close, her pulses would be shooting skywards to join the stars.

Carrie closed her eyes and bit her lip. The meal had been perfect, the wine sweetly aromatic, the atmosphere heady and all she could think of was *him*.

'What's wrong?' Howard asked irritably.

Carrie opened her eyes and levelled her gaze at him.

'I think tonight was a mistake,' she murmured. 'I thought we could be sensible about the whole thing but we can't, can we?'

He reached out and grasped her fingers across the table. 'I'd hoped we might get back together.'

'Oh, Howard, you know that's impossible.'

'It was losing that first job that did it, wasn't it?' He gulped more wine and Carrie's heart sank. He was drinking far too much, it was a long drive back and he was starting to sound morose.

'I think we ought to go, Howard.' She stood and picked up her clutch bag from the table.

'You didn't want to know because I was out of work.' He stood up with her, threw money for the bill on the table. 'That's why I didn't write and tell you about the Puerto job. I knew what you'd say, what you'd think. Kick a man when he's down.'

Embarrassed, Carrie walked away. People were beginning to stare. Howard caught up with her in the car park, swung her round.

'That's it, I suppose? There's no room for failure in your life, is there?' he blazed angrily.

'Stop that pity-me attitude, Howard, and we might be able to discuss this properly! You wanted to come here to Spain and as it turns out it's the best thing that has happened to you. You're successful now but it doesn't change how I feel about you. It had nothing to do with you losing your job, it just happened to coincide with our changing feelings for each other.'

All the life seemed to drain out of him and he raked a weary hand through his corn-coloured hair.

'I suppose you're right,' he admitted, and Carrie breathed a sigh of relief. She didn't want a blazing row; she'd seen enough of those back in England, that dreadful month before he had come out to Spain.

He unlocked the passenger door of the car for her. Well, at least he wasn't going to leave her stranded. She got in, waited till they were heading back down the hillside before speaking.

'I'm really sorry for the way things have turned out for us, Howard, but I'm pleased you've settled. In years to come we'll probably hoot over this. It's an amazing coincidence we've both ended up working for Alexander Drayton, isn't it?'

She wondered what she had said to offend him this time because with a screech of brakes he pulled up at the side of the road in a swirl of furious dirt.

'That's what all this is about, isn't it? To hell with changed feelings, it's him!' Howard ground out, fingers white around the steering-wheel.

'What are you talking about?' she gasped, swivelling in her seat to glare at him.

'I suppose you're after bigger fish now,' he said cruelly. 'Well, go for it, Carrie—with your looks you're in with a chance. I've seen the way he looks at you . . .'

She hit him then, only lightly across the side of his face with her straw clutch bag, but enough to show him the contempt she held for a remark like that.

'Don't you ever hint at anything like that again, Howard,' she seethed between clenched teeth. 'It was a spiteful thing to suggest and doesn't score you any sympathy votes. I'm not interested in the man in that way at all. Drive me back to the Marina.'

Without a word of apology he did just that, drove as if the devil was on his tail. No pretence this time, he screeched to a halt in the parking bay outside her apartment. It was Carrie who sighed with relief because Alex's car wasn't there.

She got out quickly, and slammed the door behind her. She hurried round to the pavement and Howard's arm snaked through the open window and grabbed at her.

'Aren't you going to thank me for a lovely evening?' he bit sarcastically.

Wincing with pain as Howard's grip tightened, she mumbled a thank-you and tried to pull away.

'You can do better than that, darling.' With an excruciating wrench he pulled her half in the car. His mouth was hard and cold on hers and with a strength drawn from fear she tore herself away. He revved the engine in a feeble macho attempt to show her she hadn't won.

'Goodnight, *sweetheart*.' He emphasised the word cruelly, and then pulled away with a screech of burning rubber on asphalt.

Carrie stood where she was, too stupefied to move. She should never have agreed to dine with him—now there was bitterness and she hadn't wanted that. As for the suggestion she was after Alexander Drayton...and what did Howard mean, he'd seen the way Alex looked at her? She knew Alexander Drayton wanted her but was he showing his desire in public? With a deep shudder she walked round the corner to the apartment entrance.

'Is Benson pestering you?' A voice came from the deep shadows. Alexander Drayton stepped into the light of the entrance hall.

Carrie's eyes shot past him to the white Mercedes at the side-entrance. He'd never parked there before. Why tonight of all nights?

'No...I...' Her voice petered out. There was really nothing to say. If she told the truth it would open up territories Howard wouldn't thank her for.

'I had a shrewd idea there was something going on between you two,' he said lazily, stepping towards her.

He knew! Carrie blinked fearfully. 'How?' she murmured.

'It was quite easy really. You're a beautiful woman, men look and look again. Benson didn't. He seemed impervious to your considerable charms.' His hungry eyes raked over her, leaving no doubt what he meant by that. Carrie felt as naked as the first time they had met.

'My suspicions were aroused the time you first met each other in the restaurant,' he went on. 'You acted as if you'd had the life knocked out of you. Since then I've watched the pair of you. His eyes looking through you, yours always averted. It was obvious you were both trying to hide your attraction for each other.' He stood in front of her, shirt sleeves up over his elbows, his suit jacket held carelessly over one shoulder. 'So what went wrong tonight? Did your conscience suddenly get in the way? When Benson thought he was home and dry did you suddenly scream "fiancé" and come over coyly Victorian?'

'What the hell do you mean?' she blurted furiously. Then she saw it, in a blinding flash she understood, but it was ten times worse. He *didn't* know about her and Howard but he thought she had been leading him on!

'I'm not surprised he sounded so bitter and drove off as if the devil was after him. I know how he feels. I've suffered at the hands of the she-devil too.'

Oh, God! This was awful! He believed she'd done the same to Howard as she'd done to him that night in the scented walkway. Tears of desperation sprang to her eyes. She'd rather he knew the truth about her and Howard, anything rather than being thought a teasing tramp.

'It's not what you think Alex. Howard and I aren't having an affair——'

'I know that,' he said drily. 'If you were he wouldn't have driven off in such desperation. But I hardly think you were fair to the man. You led him on——'

'What! By accepting a dinner invitation?' Fury rose in her. She'd had a dreadful night with Howard and now this. She didn't deserve it. 'And I didn't lead you on in the scented walkway either...' She stopped, the colour draining from her face. The scented walkway! It came out sounding vaguely romantic, as if she'd given it considerable thought, which she hadn't.

He smiled cynically. 'I wonder if you know exactly what you are doing or if you are genuinely as naïve as you sometimes appear. I said you were an enigma and you are.'

'Wild gypsy! She-devil! Enigma!' she defied him. 'Would that I were! I wouldn't be wasting my time with this silly conversation, would I? I'd be soaking up the sun somewhere far more exotic than the Marina del Oro!' She stepped forward to push through the doors but Alex halted her, his hand gripping her forearm.

'With some millionaire, no doubt?' he knifed sharply.

'Probably!' she snapped and then it was out before she could stop it. 'Doing a Fiona!'

His eyes darkened furiously and Carrie wished she could take back those words. She saw the hurt, in that moment knew that Fiona had meant more to him than he had admitted.

'Maybe that's what you're all about,' he grated back at her, letting go of her arm. 'It's not uncommon for secretaries to work their feminine wiles on their unsuspecting bosses.'

Carrie laughed then, more in hysteria than mirth. 'I do believe I'm working for a contender for the title of chauvinist pig of the world!' Her laughter died and the anger that stepped in was uncontrollable. 'How dare you? How dare you make such an assumption? I have no interest in you whatsoever and if I had it wouldn't be because of your wealth. I'm not a damned enigma, Alexander Drayton. I'm quite straightforward if you took the trouble to look at me and not through Fiona-tainted eyes either. I'm a secretary, a working girl. I'm as simple as that.' She drew breath, dark eyes warring with his. 'I don't need this sort of hassle. With my qualifications I can work for who I choose and from now on I don't choose to work for you!'

She stormed into the apartment building, fled up the marble stairway, fumbling in her bag for the keys. They fell to the ground with a clink and Alexander Drayton was there to pick them up. Taking her by the elbow, he held her firmly while he unlocked the door, and pushed her not so gently into her apartment.

'Make some coffee,' he ordered, tossing his jacket over the back of a chair.

'Make it yourself!' she hissed. 'As from this moment I don't work for you any more!'

She thought he would hit her, such was the depth of his fury. Unable to face it, she ran to the bedroom and dragged her suitcase from the wardrobe. She was going. She didn't need this pressure, she wouldn't stand for it!

'You're going nowhere!' he thundered from the doorway. 'So get that damned case unpacked this minute.'

Her back to him, she seethed over her shoulder. 'No way. I'm going and that's final!'

She heard his sharp intake of breath and her head twisted to face him, half afraid he might resort to violence. She didn't see violence in his hooded gaze—no, not violence but a grim determination that she wouldn't have her own way, at any price.

'You walk out of this job and you'll never work again, I promise you,' he said with such deliberation that she believed him.

'You'd do that, would you?' she whispered huskily. 'You're an even bigger bastard than I thought you were.' She turned away from him. Suddenly the fight drained from her. She resumed her packing with a resigned air. He could do what he liked, blacklist her with every agency in the world, she didn't care any more, she just wanted to get away from here and from him.

He came behind her, took her by the shoulders and turned her to him. His mouth closed over hers immediately. A single kiss that proved to her she did care, painfully so, but what did it say of him? She blinked open her eyes as he drew away from her, tried to understand the look in his eyes, that grim set of his jaw. No anger—that had sagged out of his body as their lips had met—so what was he trying to prove to both of them by kissing her that way?

'I'm going to make some coffee, so be a good girl and unpack,' he said quietly.

'Don't patronise me!' she blurted, her last burst of spirit. She was suddenly tired, so completely exhausted that she wanted to sleep for a week.

He shrugged his shoulders from the doorway. 'I can't win with you, can I?'

She sat on the edge of the bed and listened to him clattering around in the kitchen. Knowing the man, the sounds were unnatural. He's not going to let me leave, but why? she considered. Fool, she told herself. Where was he going to get another secretary at such short notice? She got up from the bed, raking her fingers through her tousled mane. She bristled at the thought of that kiss, executed with such expertise, no doubt to lower her resistance. Did he think one kiss would change her mind? It very nearly had, but no, she wasn't as gullible as he thought.

'I've not changed my mind,' she told him from the kitchen doorway. He was laying a tray of coffee and biscuits.

'I've not changed mine either,' he told her flatly. 'You're not leaving and that's that.'

So it was war, was it? Well, she would win, on that she was determined. He couldn't make her stay!

She moved out of the way as he lifted the tray, and followed him into the sitting area.

They sat opposite each other. 'I can't work under this pressure,' she murmured over her coffee-cup. Suddenly the steam evaporated from her. She didn't want a fight. She wanted peace and some sort of truce, though that was hardly likely with Alex. Compromise wasn't one of his virtues.

'You said you were used to it.'

'The work isn't a problem.'

How could she say what was on her mind? It was him not the job. Tonight, out with Howard in that little Spanish restaurant, watching the dancers, she had felt an envy deep inside her. She had wanted to be one of those lovers swaying closely to the music. But not with Howard or any other man but him, this man sprawled in the chair across from her.

'We are the problem, aren't we?' he offered quietly.

'I don't know what you mean.'

She did of course, knew the very heart of the problem. Couldn't admit it to him, admit that every time he took her in his arms something so wonderful and strange and exciting happened inside her that most rational thought fled. It would be easy to have an affair with him and someone lesser than herself would probably be in the throes of it at this very moment. But Carrie couldn't because the little spark of rationality that remained told her that for him it would be just another affair.

'Oh, we've switched to Little Miss Naïveté now, have we?' He picked up a biscuit and bit into it. 'Excuse me, but I haven't eaten tonight.'

Her heart panged at the thought that he had no one waiting for him after a hard day's work. She dismissed such a thought. Alexander Drayton was a survivor, could well look after himself.

'I'm not being intentionally naïve,' she told him quietly, 'but you do tend to talk in riddles.'

He shrugged. 'Perhaps I expect you to be sophisticated enough to read them.'

'There you go again.'

He smiled and brushed the crumbs from his fingers. 'You're right. Let's put it out in the open, shall we? You're my secretary, a damned good one too, and I'm your boss, a damned good one too.' She smiled unwillingly at that. 'The problem arises because we want to make love to each other.'

Carrie blinked her wide eyes in shock, gasped and lost her voice.

'I think you must be mistaken,' she croaked when her voice came back. How could he be so coldly callous?

'Mistaken about my own feelings?' he drawled. 'I think not.' He was teasing and Carrie's anger bubbled again. Never in her life had she met anyone who could arouse her fury so swiftly and with such little effort.

'You've got it wrong,' she blurted. 'Got it wrong about *my* feelings.' He seemed to think she felt the same way, that their problem was a sexual one and if that was overcome all would be plain sailing from then on. It might be for him but Carrie knew in her heart it would be a disaster for her, her love-life couldn't be so transient.

'Have I?' He raised a derisive dark brow. 'You melt in my arms.'

Carrie shot to her feet. She needed air. She lurched to the patio doors and slid them open with such force that they shuddered. She stepped out and drew in a breath of warm night air.

'Don't touch me!' she grated as she felt the heat of his body behind her. He came and stood next to her, powerful hands wrapped around the wrought-iron balustrade.

'I won't touch you,' he promised, so sensually that it was as if he already had. 'Because I don't want to hurt you any more.'

'You know you are hurting me yet you still go on with it,' she said softly. 'You know I'm ... I'm engaged and yet you——' Yes, she would use that. Her engagement. He wasn't to know it was over. It might be her saviour.

'Because I'm curious,' he interrupted. 'You fell into my arms the night I took you out to dinner.'

'Look,' she sighed, 'I need to explain. I wasn't lying about being afraid.' She wouldn't tell him she'd been with Howard but she *had* to make him try and understand. 'I'd been for a walk and I got lost. All the walkways look the same at night. I panicked and nearly fell down a flight of steps, then I thought I heard a footstep. I was so frightened I fell into your arms ... I ... I suppose what happened next was inevitable.' She bit her lip hard. 'I'm not that sort of girl,' she went on in a strained whisper. 'You ... you see, there were problems with

my fiancé, before I came out to Spain. I was confused, thinking about him.'

'And you needed someone. I wasn't far wrong,
was I? Anyone would have done.'

'No!' Carrie stated emphatically. 'No, it wasn't
like that at all.' She wasn't sure, though. Maybe
stretched out on a psychiatrist's couch she might
admit that she had needed someone to love that
night, someone to make love to her, emotionally
and physically. But she wasn't on that couch and
she couldn't admit to anything at the moment. Not
to him. 'I was just relieved I'd crashed into you.
At the moment of impact I felt safe.'

'And then...' he urged softly.

Carrie drew her arms around her for comfort.
'I...don't know what came over me...' She re-
lived every kiss, every caress, every pulse that had
careered wildly inside her. She prayed he wouldn't
attempt to repeat it because she wasn't responsible
any more. With him her reservations could so easily
be crushed in the stampede of her emotions.

It was a long while before he spoke. 'You don't
know yourself, do you?' he breathed despondently.
'You have these emotions raging through you and
you haven't a clue what they are all about.'

'You sound disappointed.' She lifted her chin,
eyes glinting like silver in the moonlight.

'In one way I am,' he said on a sigh. 'I can't take
advantage of such innocence, can I? I'm tempted
to take you in my arms at this very moment, to
make love to you tonight, but it would be unfair,
to us both. I'll just have to be patient and wait.'
He paused before adding, 'Yes, the waiting could
be interesting.'

'Waiting?' she husked, turning to look at his dark features bathed in silver from the moon over the bay.

'Waiting for you to realise just what you do want.' Slowly he lifted his hand, drew a wisp of silky hair from her cheek. His fingers lingered on her skin, caressing the warmth of it.

Carrie didn't stop him, didn't want to, just held her breath as the world stopped whirling, leaving her motionless in that vacuum again.

He started to quote Garcia Lorca, in a voice that was so mesmeric that she closed her eyes.

She stood on her balcony for what seemed like a lifetime after he left. As the full moon shifted restlessly through the night sky she felt the urge to run and run like a wild gypsy, but from what she wasn't sure. Maybe Alex, maybe herself.

She drew in a deep breath of perfumed air which did nothing to help her, only served to remind her that the gypsy in her soul had risen that night in the scented walkway and if she stayed in Andalucía with Alex was sure to rise again.

So why wasn't she running? She closed her tear-filled eyes and gripped the balcony edge for strength. Was she the enigma he said she was, the she-devil who drove men wild? If she knew for certain she'd start running now and never stop. But she wasn't sure. Thanks to Alexander Drayton she was sure of nothing any more.

CHAPTER FIVE

'WHAT are you doing with Alex's jacket?'

Carrie whirled in the corridor. Adela had come up behind her, as stealthy as a jungle cat.

'Returning it to him,' she said quickly and carried on walking to her office. He'd left it in her apartment last night and she hadn't discovered it till this morning. She'd tapped on his apartment door before leaving for the office but he'd already left.

Adela followed her into the office and watched with curious eyes as Carrie shook it out and hung it in the closet. She guessed that Adela was dying to know more but pride wouldn't allow her another question.

'Do you want to see Alex?' She hoped she didn't because she wanted to see him first.

'No, you actually.'

Carrie looked up from the mail on her desk in surprise, a slight chill running down her spine. Adela had not been around much lately. Whether or not Alex was tiring of her she wasn't to know, but the affair that she suspected and Howard had confirmed seemed to be a pretty feeble one. Even that night when her power had failed, the night he was expecting Adela, had turned out to be half an hour of business chat accompanied by the clink of glasses and then Adela had left. Not that Carrie had been listening intentionally, but noise carried outside in the night air.

'I came to ask you if you can do a session downstairs in Sales tomorrow?'

'I'm sorry, it would be out of the question.' She smiled sweetly. She was about to add she wouldn't be here but Alex came out of his office, reminding her that she owed it to him to tell him first.

'I agree, it's out of the question, Adela. Get Benson to organise his rota more efficiently. I'm not having my secretary doing his work for him.'

'Howard is tied up with this Japanese deal, Alex—he's hard pressed as it is. It's coming up for August and the Marina will be packed with tourists——'

'And tourists can't afford property here, Adela.'

Her black eyes narrowed furiously and Carrie understood why these two seemed to be forever falling out. Adela's character was as strong as Alex's. She didn't like being crossed and was used to having her own way, just like him. 'When I worked for Puerto del Sol——'

'You're working for Marina del Oro now,' Alex interrupted firmly. 'And we have already established that the tourist wandering in off the street is a timewaster.' He turned to Carrie and handed her a sheet of paper. 'Fax this to Dybarts in Geneva, Carrie. In my office, Adela.'

Carrie fed the fax, stamping out the code impatiently. Adela had for the moment thwarted her resignation plans. She frowned. That was interesting, though; Adela had worked for Puerto del Sol. She must have been the only trustworthy person Alex had kept on. So Howard and Adela

must have known each other before. Was she the
one who had tipped him off that all was not well
with the company? As the legal adviser she must
have had her finger on the financial pulse. Funny
that Adela should show such allegiance to Howard
when she was intimately involved with Alex, but of
course Howard did have a certain charm, sometimes! It seemed that her suspicions of a romantic
triangle weren't far wrong.

A reply to the fax came through and with a sigh
Carrie attended to it. She had it in her hand when
Adela and Alex came out of the office. They were
laughing and Alex's hand was on Adela's shoulder.
Carrie's heart twisted unexpectedly.

'Dybarts?' Alex asked, eyes flicking to the piece
of paper in Carrie's hand. Carrie nodded. 'I'll see
you later, Adela. Make it about six for a drink. I
want to get going by seven.'

He turned into his office, motioning Carrie to
follow. Adela left, looking well pleased with herself,
and Carrie wondered where Alex was taking her
tonight. If only Adela had been a fly on the wall
last night when Alex had admitted he had wanted
to make love to her. Would she still be looking so
smugly satisfied?

Carrie waited till Alex read the fax before
speaking. 'I know my contract says I should give
a month's notice but I think in the circumstances
I should go right away.'

He leaned back on his desk to study her. 'Oh,
you do, do you?' he drawled. His eyes raked her
from head to toe and then he smiled. 'And what
do you hope to achieve by this little performance?'

She knew exactly what he meant. This morning she had deliberately played herself down, screwed her hair into a tight bun at the nape of her neck, not bothered with make-up and though she was melting in the heat she had dressed in a severe, long-sleeved shirt worn loosely over the sternest skirt she had with her, navy-blue linen.

'Don't forget I know exactly what's under that lot,' he grinned. 'You could wear a turnip sack and it wouldn't play down your sexuality. Now, what's this about leaving? I do believe I've heard this tape before.'

She was furious before she started but fury got her nowhere with Alexander Drayton. Swallowing hard, she said, 'You obviously didn't get the message and I'm getting a bit tired of repeating it. I want to leave.'

'I know you do and I've already told you that it's impossible.'

'Yet you make it impossible for me to stay. Just now you referred to my sexuality. You can't forget it, can you?' She held his gaze deliberately, to show him she wasn't playing games.

Folding his arms across his chest, he let out a sigh. 'You make it difficult, Carrie. The very idea of dressing yourself down today says that you are aware of your own sexuality and the effect it has on me and yet——'

'Please stop!' She kneaded her brow irritably.

'I'm sorry. I'm teasing you and you're very serious this morning, aren't you?'

'Yes, I am. I think it best I leave,' she murmured, fixing her eyes on the carpet at his feet.

'I need you, Carrie,' he said smoothly. 'And I mean I need a secretary more than a mistress at the moment.'

Her eyes flicked up. Of course, Adela was flavour of the month again, wasn't she?

'You shouldn't have any trouble replacing me. There must be a thousand girls out there willing to work in the sun for a couple of months,' she argued.

'I don't want a thousand girls. I want you. We work well together, you can't deny that.'

She couldn't. The office hours went smoothly— it was the other hours that were giving her trouble. What was wrong with her that she couldn't cope with the situation? Deep, deep down she had an idea why but the thought was too scary to dredge up.

'I thought last night we had reached a point of understanding,' he went on.

Carrie shrugged. 'In a way, so did I, but I didn't sleep very well and... and then this morning...'

'You thought it best to leave,' he finished for her. Slowly he reached out and lifted her hand. With finger and thumb he rubbed the space where her engagement ring had been. 'Has this anything to do with your decision? Do you want to go back to England to patch it up with your fiancé?'

Guilt stabbed at her for not telling him the truth about Howard. But it didn't matter now anyway.

'I'm not engaged any more,' she told him with a small smile. 'You were right about me. I don't know myself yet. It wouldn't be fair to either of us to continue a relationship that I was unsure about.'

'I agree. You need to be sure.'

Carrie drew her fingers from his, the tone of his voice causing her hands to tremble as she did so. You need to be sure. Those words had sounded meaningful, as if he'd learnt the true value of them for himself.

He walked round the side of his desk. 'I don't want to force you to stay, Carrie, but you'll put me in a hell of a fix if you go.'

If emotional blackmail wasn't a form of force she didn't know what was!

'I really have found you indispensable. You're probably the best secretary——'

'And flattery is supposed to get you anywhere, is it?' Carrie felt herself unwillingly weakening.

Slumping down into his chair, he raked a hand through his hair. 'The Japanese are arriving at the end of the month, I have meetings in Madrid with the Banco de Bilbao, I have three French industrialists expecting me in Paris, then there's Geneva——'

'Stop!' Carrie said on a sigh of resignation. 'OK, I'll stay.' She didn't say any more—it would be useless putting conditions to Alexander Drayton. I'll stay if you promise not to drive me wild with your kisses . . .

'No conditions?' he enquired coolly, gazing at her from under hooded brows.

How easily he could read her. The thought was frightening.

'No point,' she said stiffly, gathering up a pile of papers from his desk. 'You wouldn't abide by them. Leopards and spots and all that!'

He laughed as she walked to the door. 'Oh, by the way, be ready by seven.'

She swung to face him. Surely he was taking Adela out?

'Ready for what?' she asked, instantly wishing she hadn't said that. If she was to carry on working for him she would have to be more stringent in her choice of words.

'A trip—and pack enough for a few days.' His head was already bent over files on his desk.

Pressing the papers tightly to her chest to still her pounding heartbeat, she managed, 'A few days where?'

'Gibraltar. There's a one-day investment seminar I wish to attend. Don't forget to pack your passport.'

'If it's a one-day seminar we could be there and back in the helicopter!'

He looked up. 'The rest of the trip will be pleasure, Carrie, so pack something more exciting than a turnip sack!'

The phone rang and the thought raged through her that he must have some arrangement with the telephone company to call at the most inopportune moments. She closed the door behind her, biting her lip with such force that she thought she would draw blood.

Pressure of work prevented her asking more about the trip that morning. She tried to put it out of her mind and concentrate on her work but it was hard. She made several mistakes on the computer, none serious, but they could have been, she reprimanded herself.

She was relieved when two o'clock came and Alex said they had finished for the day and he didn't expect her back at five.

'Try and get some rest this afternoon; we have a long drive ahead of us tonight. Seven sharp.'

'We're driving to Gibraltar?' She guessed it would take some hours.

'Yes, and we're going on to Cordoba the next day.'

'Cordoba?' she echoed.

'Yes, Cordoba,' he clipped and walked out of the office.

To her knowledge he had no business contacts in Cordoba so why should he want to go there? Was this the pleasure part of the trip? He'd admitted he wanted her, so was he planning on seducing her there, away from Adela? She smiled at the idiotic thought. Alexander Drayton wasn't the sort of man to go to such lengths for a flirtation with his secretary.

Packing up the portable computer for the trip, she considered that since coming to Spain she had discovered a lot about herself. True, she was still a little confused about some aspects, but one thing she was sure of: an affair with Alexander Drayton would be foolish and dangerous but it was all down to her. If she was smart enough she could avoid it. She doubted very much if rape was one of his vices.

Later, she swam lazily in the pool behind the apartments. No fear of Alex interrupting her; she'd seen him drive off with Enrique the architect.

A body dived in next to her, surfaced and swam beside her. Carrie blinked water from her eyes and struck out for the edge of the pool.

'Howard! What are you doing here?' She hauled herself out and sat on the side with her legs dangling in the water. She hoped he wasn't going to make a nuisance of himself—she'd had more than enough from him.

'Eating humble pie.' He snatched at her legs and she kicked water. He laughed, swam away and Carrie watched him curiously, her eyes narrowed against the glare of the sun on the water.

He swam a couple of lengths then joined her, raking his fingers through his hair to get rid of the excess water.

'I'm sorry about the other night. I was rude to you. It's just that I couldn't accept that we're finally finished.'

'Howard,' Carrie cried in exasperation, 'don't let's talk about it any more. Let's put our relationship where it belongs, in the past.'

'You're right. I suppose I had too much to drink and was feeling a bit low.'

'I understand and I forgive you, but, Howard, for both our sakes, take it easy. Your little display of temper was witnessed last night.'

'What do you mean?' he croaked.

'Alex saw us together.'

'God! You didn't let on——?'

'Don't panic,' Carrie husked irritably. 'Your skin is safe. He saw us when we arrived back last night. Said he'd guessed something was going on because of our indifference to each other. It aroused his suspicions.'

'You didn't say we knew each other before?'

'Of course not! Though for the life of me I don't know why I didn't tell him the truth. He seemed to think it a bit off that I have a fiancé at home in England and yet I was out with you. Doesn't say much for my morals, does it?' she huffed. 'And another thing. You didn't tell me you knew Adela before.'

'What the hell are you talking about?' His reaction was so violent that Carrie flinched.

'Adela worked for Puerto del Sol. You must have known her.' She frowned, oddly sensing that whatever Howard said next would hardly satisfy her.

'Hundreds of people worked for them.' He shrugged. 'She might have done. I can't recall her.' Abruptly, too abruptly, he hauled himself to his feet, snatched his towel from a chair. 'I'd better get going. I've some work to catch up on.'

She watched him go, the towel flung carelessly around his neck, his shoulders slumped, her intuition warning her that he had lied to her. He had looked scared, just for a fleeting second he had shown real fear. Sliding back into the water to cool off, Carrie started swimming, slowly, effortlessly, trying to reason Howard out. Was he so terrified of losing this job if Alex found he had worked for that corrupt company? She wondered if Howard had perhaps been involved in those shady sales deals. She dismissed that thought with a pang of conscience for even considering it. Howard wasn't dishonest, on that she would stake her life, and of course Adela must know that too. She would never have let Alex take him on if she had suspected any such thing.

Still, it was a bit of a mystery, his denying he knew her when it was pretty certain he must have done. And she didn't totally believe that excuse that it was business they were discussing that night she had seen them in the restaurant. If it had been Marina del Oro business there had been no reason for her to disappear the way she had done. The pair of them were hiding something from Alex. If it was an affair that could be even more tricky for Howard than the Puerto del Sol business! She let out a sigh and wearily climbed out of the pool. A sleep for an hour or so seemed like a nice idea.

She had a headache when she woke, took an aspirin with a glass of water and started to pack. She smiled at the dresses she folded into her case. Emerald silk, fine black lace, spicy Indian cotton—hardly turnip sacks any of them.

She opted for a cool cerise pink cotton dress to travel in and matching espadrilles, and because of his derisive comments about dressing herself down she defiantly brushed her hair loose and allowed herself some make-up. She gathered up her toilet bag and that was the last thing she pushed into her case.

It was as she struggled out of her apartment with her case that she came face to face with Adela, who had obviously just left Alex. Her lovely dark eyes were narrowed as if she'd suddenly been given bad news and Carrie wondered if Alex had just told her she was accompanying him on his trip.

'All ready, are you?' Adela smiled so sweetly that Carrie was immediately on the defensive. She had reason to be. The smile soon dropped from Adela's face. 'Just remember your position.'

'I beg your pardon?'

'You're a secretary, Carrie, and always will be; don't forget it.'

She clicked off down the corridor, leaving Carrie with a flush on her face. So Adela wasn't overjoyed that Alex was taking her to Gibraltar, but that had sounded like a warning!

'Good grief. I said pack enough for a few days, not weeks,' Alex commented as he loaded her case into the boot.

'I'm sorry...' She felt the colour rising to her face.

'It was a joke, Carrie,' he assured her, taking the computer from her hand and putting it on the back seat of the car. 'Get in.'

She sat stiffly at first but relaxed after a while. The car was miraculously cool and the highway that ran alongside the coastline smooth. Alex spoke once or twice, mainly to point out a town or village that he thought might interest her, otherwise there was little exchange between them. After an hour or so Carrie could contain herself no longer. She'd tried to dismiss it from her mind but she simply couldn't.

'Adela reminded me of my position just before we left.'

'What position is that?' Alex asked casually.

'A secretary. Said I always will be and not to forget it.'

Alex threw back his head and laughed. 'Coming from Adela that sounds remarkably like a gypsy's warning.' He reached across and tapped her knee. 'Don't lose any sleep over it. It's killing her knowing I'm taking you with me this trip. She's a very jealous lady.'

'She has reason to be, does she?' Carrie prompted, not sure that she wasn't playing with fire but thinking it worth the risk.

'Every reason. She knows you have more chance of getting me into bed than she does.'

Cheeks flaming, Carrie stared bleaky out of the side window. 'I suppose I asked for that,' she mumbled regretfully.

'You did rather,' he chuckled.

'Is it true, then?' Her cheeks remained aflame. 'I don't mean...I mean...' She took a deep breath. 'What I'm trying to say is, is it true that you haven't...? I mean...'

'Am I having an affair with her? Is that what you are struggling to get out?' He grew suddenly serious. 'Do you think I would be the way I am with you if I were having an affair with another woman?'

Carrie couldn't look at him. 'That isn't an answer,' she blurted.

'It is if you take the trouble to unravel it.'

'I'm not into riddles, remember?' she retorted.

They drove on in silence. Carrie miserably regretting she had ever brought the subject up. And why had she anyway? Stupid thought. Ever since meeting the lovely Adela she had been curious to know what sort of a relationship she had with Alex. Well, now she knew. And would Alex misinterpret her curiosity and think she was jealous? Served her right if he did; she should have kept her mouth shut!

Alex spoke at last, as it was getting dark.

'Are you hungry?'

She was starving. 'Yes, actually I am.' She stretched. 'Tired too.'

Suddenly a horrible thought crossed her mind. 'I didn't book a hotel!' she cried, turning to him in dismay. Damn, what sort of secretary was she?

He laughed at her appalled expression. 'It's all taken care of.'

'But I should have done it, that's what I'm paid for!' she wailed.

'Well, I did rather spring it on you. We're staying at the Holiday Inn and it was booked months ago anyway so don't feel guilty about it.'

She did feel guilty nevertheless. She should have thought of the accommodation before they were practically there. She was slipping, losing her grip on her position.

'What about Cordoba?'

'That's taken care of too.'

'Great,' Carrie moaned, tightening her fists into balls beside her. 'Who needs a secretary?'

'I do,' he laughed. 'I'd forgotten the computer.'

She relaxed, laughed with him, vowed not to make such a silly mistake again. Alex was in a good humour but the next time she slipped up he might not take it so casually.

'Before we cross the border into Gib, are you a fish person or not?'

'Do you mean do I like fish? I love it.'

Immediately he took a side turning off the main highway, drove carefully through the narrow streets of a coastal village till they came out almost directly on to a beach.

It looked as if a fiesta was about to begin. Brightly painted fishing boats were drawn up on to the beach and crowds were gathered round each boat as the catch, in baskets, was thrown down on to the sand.

All along the beach olive-wood fires were burning and local women raked the hot ashes.

'Will grilled sardines suit you?' he asked as, grasping her hand, he led her along the sands to a *merendero* with tables and chairs on the beach, flamenco music blaring from a stereo and the biggest fire of all blazing in a brazier.

She laughed as they flopped down on rickety cane chairs at an equally rickety table covered with a paper cloth. 'This is wonderful,' she cried, eyes wide and bright with excitement.

The waiter brought them a bottle of chilled white wine and a basket of fresh crusty bread.

Alex poured the wine, and watched her as she sipped it and murmured appreciatively.

'Do you like it?'

'It's wonderful and so is this bread.' She looked at him across the table. He was leaning back, wine glass in one hand, a chunk of bread in the other. He wasn't Alexander Drayton the financier at the moment. He was someone else, someone who tightened the muscles around her heart till she was breathless. His hair wasn't so sleek any more, his short-sleeved shirt was crumpled from the car, his light cotton jeans creased across his thighs. He wore white espadrilles that weren't white any longer. He looked relaxed and amused.

'What are you thinking?'

She laughed. The wine had gone straight to her head, not far enough to addle her though. 'I'm thinking that this is fun. I've never eaten on the beach before.' She averted her eyes from him to the moon silvering the sea. She would have to be careful, oh, so careful. Wine, sea, moon and him! Heady combination.

They watched as the owner of the beach bar tossed fat sardines on to the hot grill. The smell was so overwhelmingly delicious that there was a roar of approval from a crowd of Spaniards. Then the singing started, fishermen's songs delivered tunelessly in high-pitched voices.

'It's been a good catch.' Alex laughed.

They were presented with the first plateful of the barbecued fish and a crowd gathered as Alex with deft fingers ripped off the head and, tilting his head back, held the fish by its tail over his mouth, then in one movement the flesh was gone and what remained in his fingers was the complete bone and the tail.

The fishermen approved with another roar and Carrie shouted over the noise, 'You've done this before, haven't you?'

He nodded and laughed as the crowd urged her to do likewise.

'*No puedo!*' she shrieked but they clapped her on till she knew there was no escape.

She pulled off the head, tried to mimic Alex but failed miserably as the fish broke. She caught most of it in her mouth but the rest slid down her chin and landed in her lap. She didn't care that her dress was probably ruined, nor did anyone else. With more cries she was urged on till by the third fish she had got the knack. Then, satisfied, the crowd moved back to the barbecue, laughing and clapping.

'Oh, they're delicious!' she enthused.

'I thought you would enjoy this rather than a hotel meal.'

'The gypsy in me, eh?' she laughed.

'You said it, not me,' he said quietly.

She hadn't heard, she told herself, wiping the oil from her mouth with a paper serviette. She tried to sober herself but in this atmosphere it was impossible. Everyone around them was laughing or singing or swallowing whole sardines.

When they'd finished, she sat back as contented as a cat. 'I think that must rate as one of the best meals I've ever had.'

'Quite biblical, wasn't it?'

'Heavenly,' she smiled. She shook her hands in front of her. 'Messy, though.'

He nodded his dark head towards the sea. 'Anything less would be sacrilege.'

She got up and ran beside him to the water's edge. They kicked off their espadrilles and crouched down to wash the fish oil from their fingers in the frothy surf that rolled around their feet. Carrie splashed her face.

'Messy eater, aren't you?' he teased, and she reached out to overbalance him but he caught her by the wrist and together they stood up. The sea lapped their feet and it was the only movement in the whole wide world. Their eyes met for a long second.

She prayed he wouldn't and yet was disappointed when he didn't. Her lips burned as if he had.

'I think we ought to get going,' he said at last, his voice ragged in his throat. He didn't let go of her hand till they reached the car on the edge of the sand.

Gibraltar was what she needed, so British it was like a dousing of cold water on her senses. She needed sobering, she mused as they booked in at the hotel. They reached their rooms, doubles across the corridor from each other, and Carrie was still struggling to right her mind. The *merendero* on the beach had been a delicious interlude where they had laughed and eaten and drunk wine as if they were lovers. But they weren't lovers and this hotel was reality. She was here to work.

'What time do you need me in the morning?' she asked, slipping back into her secretarial role. She turned the key to open the door.

'We'll breakfast at eight and take it from there.' He smiled, the way he often did in the office. 'See you in the morning.'

She closed the door and leaned heavily against it. Tired as she was, she knew she wouldn't be able to sleep, but she must because tomorrow was just another working day.

Her dress was ruined. She stripped it off and plunged it in the washbasin to soak. She could still smell the fish and the wood ash, could still see Alex's laughing eyes across the rickety table.

Later she lay in bed and thought how formal he had sounded when he had suggested breakfast at eight. Was he being as successful as she in hiding his emotions? She'd done well, she thought, acted as naturally as possible, and so had he. But was this the waiting time? Was he just biding his time waiting for her to realise she loved him enough to go to bed with him?

With a small sob she buried her face in the crisp white pillowcase. Love. She hadn't wanted to dredge that emotion out in the open. She had hoped it would have gone away of its own free will one day. She rolled over and looked up at the ceiling. She was doing what hundreds of silly little secretaries were doing all over the globe: falling in love with their bosses. And nothing would come of it but heartbreak and signing on with another agency.

In that case I'm not going to run the risk of losing my heart or my job, she resolved. I don't want to love you and I won't! She chanted it determinedly to herself till she fell asleep.

CHAPTER SIX

'I'D LIKE to phone my father before we leave,' Carrie told Alex in the foyer of the hotel. She still couldn't believe that Alex was prepared to drive through the night after one of the most hectic days of her life.

It was one thing she had learned about Drayton the financier—when deeply involved in anything monetary his energy was boundless. He hadn't stopped all day. He had attended every lecture, talked endlessly with bankers and even found time for lengthy phone calls to Geneva, Tokyo and London. He was still on a high now. Sleep didn't warrant a mention. Carrie wanted to crawl into bed and shut her weary eyes for ever.

'Here, give him this number in Cordoba.' He scribbled a telephone number on the back of one of his business cards. 'In case of emergencies.'

Carrie smiled. She had to admit that Alex was thoughtful that way, didn't mind how many times she called her father. She hadn't taken advantage, though, just called enough times to make sure all was well.

'How are you, Dad? We're on our way to Cordoba. Have you a pen? Take the number of the hotel in case you need to call.' Carrie drummed her nails on the receiver while she waited. Typical of her father not to be able to find a pen. His coins were catalogued perfectly but the rest of his life lay in chaos around him.

'Cordoba, you say?' he muttered down the phone. 'I correspond with a dealer down there. Now, what is his name?'

'Dad,' Carrie breathed with a smile. 'Take this number, will you?' she told him gently but firmly.

'Yes, of course,' he mumbled absent-mindedly.

She repeated the number twice and then her father said. 'I remember now, Alvarez is his name. He has a fine——'

'Dad, I'll have to go,' Carrie interrupted, glancing anxiously over her shoulder. Alex was pacing like a caged tiger. If the call weren't going on the Marina del Oro account Carrie would have gladly given more time to her father.

'Yes, darling, of course. How's Gibraltar?'

Carrie laughed. 'It's strange to see British policemen walking around in this exotic setting and melting in the heat. Look, I'll call you from the hotel in Cordoba. Are you sure you're all right?' He'd been known to go all day without eating once he was buried in his coins.

'Don't worry, Mrs Burbage is keeping her beady eye on me,' he chuckled. 'Carrie?' He sounded concerned.

'Yes, Dad.'

'What exactly are you going to Cordoba for?' He might be absent-minded and a trifle eccentric but he always had her welfare to the fore.

Carrie suddenly felt icy all over. Good question. 'Oh, Alex has some business there. I'll call you tomorrow and tell you all about it. Goodbye, Dad.' She put the receiver down with tremulous fingers. Indeed, what were they going to Cordoba for?

She didn't speak till they had crossed the border into Spain and were heading north.

'Why are we going to Cordoba?'

He glanced at her briefly before setting his eyes back on the road. 'I told you—pleasure.'

'That isn't an answer.'

'It's all I'm prepared to give you at the moment.' His eyes were steadfastly ahead and Carrie could read nothing in them.

'I think you are being unfair.'

He sighed, shifted his position. 'If you really want to know, I have some business there.'

'Oh.'

'Pleasurable business,' he added with half a smile.

'Do...do you need me for this pleasurable business?' she asked hesitantly, aware she was treading a tricky path.

'Absolutely not.'

'Oh.'

He laughed. 'Is that all you can say, "Oh"?'

'I don't see the point of dragging me all over Andalucia, then,' she retorted. She was exhausted and longed for bed and this trip was going to take hours and for what?

'I couldn't do much else with you. I needed you for Gib.'

'Oh, so I'm spare baggage now, am I? So what am I supposed to do while you are off taking your pleasure?' she asked crisply.

'Well, you could shop in the market, cook for me and generally do what a good Spanish housewife does all day.'

Suddenly she was wide awake. 'What are you talking about? Shop and cook? Are you out of your mind?'

'You can cook, can't you?' he chuckled.

'Not very well as it happens, but that is beside the point. I want to know exactly what you have in mind for the next——'

'Two days,' he added for her. 'Actually I thought I was doing you a favour by getting you away from the Marina for a while. You've worked very hard since you joined us. I thought the break would do you good.'

'Shopping and cooking doesn't sound much of a break to me,' she huffed. 'And where is all this cosy domesticity going to take place?' She couldn't envisage cooking on a primus stove in some hotel room.

'In my home, of course.'

Her breath caught in her throat, hot and dry, rendering her speechless for an instant, but only for an instant.

'Your home!' she exploded. 'You live in Cordoba?' She couldn't believe it—never for a moment had she thought he would be taking her to his home.

'One of my homes,' he corrected. 'I also have a chalet in Switzerland, a penthouse in the London Docklands and a villa in the Bahamas. Sadly I spend more time in hotels than anywhere.'

'My heart bleeds for you,' Carrie muttered wickedly under her breath. She reclined her seat and tried to make herself comfortable with her back to him. 'I'm going to sleep now. Wake me when my domestic duties commence!'

He laughed in the darkness and she closed her eyes determinedly. That was it, wasn't it? He wanted her as a skivvy for a few days while he took his pleasure. Cooking and cleaning and shopping. He had to be joking! She had no intention of playing house with him!

'Carrie, wake up. We're nearly there.' He touched her arm lightly to arouse her.

Every bone in her body ached. She blinked open her eyes, which were sore and gritty. It was still dark.

'We're crossing the river Guadalquivir on the Roman stone bridge. Spectacular, isn't it?'

Could anything be remotely spectacular at this hour? Three o'clock, the dashboard clock glared back at her.

'Over there is the Mosque.'

'Impressive,' Carrie murmured sleepily.

Smoothing her hair from her face, she was suddenly assailed by guilt. She had slept while Alex had driven. He looked tired now, had obviously spent his excess energy and was looking fit to drop.

'I should have offered to drive some of the way. You must be exhausted,' she said.

'I like driving at night,' he replied.

The roads narrowed until Carrie thought the sides of white-washed houses would surely tear the wing mirrors off. The streets were picturesque and cobbled, and flowers hung from pretty wrought-iron balconies. Alex expertly manoeuvered the car into a narrow alleyway and stopped, hard up against a stone wall.

Carrie had to scramble across his seat to get out, so stiff and achy that she nearly fell out into the road. Alex scooped her up and set her on her feet with a chuckle.

'Thanks,' she mumbled, smoothing her crumpled cotton trousers and T-shirt. While Alex fetched the cases from the boot she reached inside and rescued the portable computer and her handbag from the back seat. It was only when she stood holding them in the middle of the cobbled alleyway that her head fully cleared. She gazed around her in surprise.

Tall, roughly plastered white walls rose all around her, the houses terraced and no outside indication where one house finished and another started. They were pretty with their shuttered windows and ornate balconies but it was the last place Carrie imagined Alexander Drayton the financier would live.

'Can you manage the computer and my briefcase? I'll take the cases.' He lifted them effortlessly and strode off down the narrow street, almost immediately turning left through an archway that led into a courtyard, even at night so ablaze with colourful life that Carrie gasped in surprise.

The courtyard was lit by rustic lamps attached to the rough plastered walls of the houses and at the centre of the cobbled area was a white-washed well covered with tendrils of vine and circled by terracotta pots of bright geraniums, lilies and busy Lizzies. The warm night air was scented sweetly.

'Oh, it's so pretty,' Carrie murmured, and followed Alex to an arched antique door, dark wood, heavily studded, on the far side of the courtyard. He opened it and stood back to let her enter.

She stood in the vast cool hallway which doubled as a sitting-room, her eyes acclimatising to the dimness.

Alex switched on the lights, rustic wall fittings with candle bulbs. Carrie couldn't hide her surprise and Alex laughed softly beside her.

'It isn't what you expected, is it?' he asked her.

She shook her head, gazed around her at the stark simplicity of the place. Rough white walls, dark brown clay tiles underfoot. Antique pots filled with lush green ferns, a couple of Spanish rugs of Turkish design, two simple sofas and a heavy antique book case filled to overflowing were all that furnished the room. Beyond was an open patio with planters filled with greenery, feathery palm fronds sweeping the tiles. There was a white wrought-iron table and chairs with bright cushions.

For all its simplicity it was beautiful and had a profound effect on Carrie's emotions. She was learning something new about this man, and liking it too. She was sharply aware of him standing next to her, watching her as she gazed around at his possessions. For a fearful second she fought the impulse to back out of the door because for some very odd reason the feeling that closed in around her was one of sensual sexuality. This was his home, his books, his sofas. So close to him and a part of him, an intimacy she ached to share.

She turned to him, heat rising to her cheeks at the thought that he might sense her increased pulse-rate. 'It ... it's very Spanish,' she managed to murmur. 'I ... I ... didn't imagine that this would be your taste.' She had expected a sumptuous villa. As she had tried to sleep on the drive here she had

visualised the sort of home he would have. Marble
and glass and French impressionist paintings on the
walls. These walls, apart from the rustic lights, were
bare.

'Are all your homes like this, sort of austere?'
She moved away from him, desperately trying to
sound normal. She picked up the only ornament in
the room, a carved wooden bull, put it down
quickly as it seemed to sear the flesh of her palm.

'I like to furnish my homes in keeping with their
surroundings. Hi-tech in the Docklands is fine but
would look out of place here,' he told her softly,
so softly she jerked her head to look at him, concerned to see that he looked totally exhausted.
'Come, I'll show you upstairs, the bedrooms.' His
eyes locked with hers for just an instant but long
enough to send a shiver down Carrie's spine. 'Then
I'm afraid I must sleep before I drop,' he finished,
which only slightly put Carrie's apprehension to
rest.

Alex carried the cases up the stone stairway that
coiled up from the hall and Carrie followed.

'I'll make you a drink if you like,' she suggested.
She hadn't intended to do anything by way of
housewifely duties but he was tired and she felt it
was the least she could do.

'That would be nice.'

Upstairs the rooms opened on to a gallery which
overlooked the inner patio. The gallery with its
wrought-iron balustrade was covered but above the
patio the night sky was exposed. Even then it was
hot, and Carrie thought the old house would be
unbearable without this airy inner space.

The feeling that had swamped her downstairs quadrupled upstairs. Carrie fought it feverishly, and tried not to look too intently in to his bedroom, the largest of three. He slid his case into this doorway and beckoned her to the next room and she hurried after him.

'This is your room. It overlooks the courtyard and you have your own bathroom.'

It had a double bed with an ornate carved wood headboard and a creamy lace bedspread, a matching carved wardrobe and a dressing-table and chair. There were warm rugs on mellow tiles, and the walls were bare.

Carrie crossed the stifling room and pushed open french doors on to a long balcony that ran the length of the house. She drew in fresh warm air, and closed her eyes briefly, wondering how she was going to cope for two days in this lovely old house with Alex. When she opened her eyes she saw that his room opened on to the same balcony. She didn't know whether to be alarmed by that thought or not.

'What's that lovely smell?' She breathed the heavy sweet fragrance.

He came and stood next to her in the open doorway. '*Dama de Noche*—lady of the night. It's nothing by day but at night the flowers open and fill the air with its heady perfume. Some say it smells like a Moroccan house of ill repute,' he informed her with a smile.

'I wouldn't know about that,' she uttered quickly and moved away from him, not embarrassed by his words but too aroused by the perfume and the closeness of him for comfort.

'Nor would I,' he yawned. 'If there's anything you need just wander round till you find it.' He turned to the door.

'Would you like some tea? I'll make some if you do,' she offered.

He smiled. 'As well as the perfect secretary, you sound as if you're going to be a perfect wife too. Albeit a temporary one,' he added with a mocking grin, and then, 'Yes, I'd love a cup of tea if it isn't too much trouble. You'll find all you need downstairs. I'm going to take a shower.'

The kitchen opened off the hall and from the small kitchen another door opened on to the inner patio. It was well equipped and stocked with all the basics, but nothing as sophisticated as a dishwasher or a microwave. Carrie ran her hot fingers over the cool marble worktops and puzzled over the Cordoban townhouse. It was full of old-world character and Spanish charm but hardly the residence expected of an international financier. But did Alex come up to expectation in any way?

He'd said she was an enigma. He wasn't far short of one himself. He could afford a *hacienda* in this part of the world yet he chose a simple abode that probably wasn't any different from the others opening into the courtyard.

She found everything she needed to make two mugs of tea and carried them upstairs, placing hers on an old wicker table outside his room. His door was open, but nevertheless she tapped lightly on it. She didn't want to catch him getting out of the shower. There was no answer and she peered round the door cautiously.

He lay motionless on a huge bed similar to her own. He was on his stomach, his face to one side on the pillow, his naked body covered to the waist by a white sheet.

There was no fear of him waking, his breathing was so deep and regular, so Carrie stood over him, watching him sleep peacefully. His hair, still damp from the shower, showed a tendency to curl around his ears; dark lashes, too long and thick for a man, dusted his cheek. His back was darkly bronzed and, though at rest, couldn't deny its muscular strength.

Carrie placed the mug of tea on the bedside table and then clenched her fists into balls at her side to prevent herself from reaching out and smoothing her palm across his back. She was dismayed to find that she shook with the effort of control. He was beautiful, like an animal of the jungle, full of sleek, predatory power, even in sleep a dangerous threat. The need for him was achingly heady and for a moment she allowed herself the sweet pleasure of indulgence, fantasised herself into the role of his mistress, his wife. She bit her lip fiercely. What had Adela said? 'You're a secretary, Carrie, and always will be; don't forget it.' How could she ever forget a warning like that?

Alex had brought her here to extend those secretarial duties to domestic ones. She couldn't lose sight of the fact that he was her employer and was paying her for all this and yet . . . and yet she could dream, couldn't she?

Carrie went slowly to her room, her heart aching painfully. She drank her tea and then unpacked, showered and sat out on the balcony enjoying the fragrant warm night air till she became drowsy with disturbing thoughts of the man sleeping so peacefully in the next room. So close, and yet a million miles away in availability. Later, she crawled in to bed and covered her head with the sheet.

'You really are serious, aren't you?' she bit out, waving the piece of paper he had handed her in the air.

He looked up from pouring the coffee. They were outside, sitting at the small white table on the patio. It was cool and shady, the sun not yet high enough to cause any trouble, but Carrie wasn't cool. She had slept badly, fitfully, and had woken to the sound of every motorbike in the world buzzing noisily up and down the narrow streets and every Spanish mother in the world screaming at her children.

'Quite a temper you have in the mornings,' he said drily as he poured coffee for her.

'I've been bitten to death,' she grumbled, rubbing her ankles. The mosquitoes had had a banquet at her expense in the night. Thank heavens she'd covered her face with a sheet before falling asleep.

'You'll find some cream in your bathroom cabinet and an aerosol spray. I suggest you spray your bedroom an hour or so before you retire.'

'And what about the ozone layer?' she snapped back.

'Get bitten, then,' he drawled lazily, refusing to be drawn into an argument. 'Now, what are you grizzling about, my shopping list?'

He'd handed it to her almost as soon as she had sat down to breakfast: coffee and warm rolls he had prepared while she had slept. Carrie was in no mood to appreciate that he had risen early to shop for the fresh bread and milk for the coffee.

'You really do expect me to shop and cook for you!' she challenged indignantly.

'No, I don't expect it. If you don't want to do it, don't. We can eat out. I just thought it would make a change from hotel and restaurant food. I travel so much I get sick of it. I enjoy home cooking.'

'You won't enjoy mine!'

She gulped at her coffee, ignoring the crusty rolls that looked so tempting, but she wouldn't be able to eat for the tightness in her throat. She wasn't ill, just sick at the thought of sharing his home for these two days. She wouldn't be able to bear it, she just wouldn't.

'You shop and I'll cook, then, if you object so strongly,' he said tightly.

She felt awful then, guilty, and annoyed too that he should make her feel that way.

When she didn't say anything he went on. 'Or, as I say, we can eat out.' He shrugged his big shoulders, the shoulders she had been so tempted to caress the night before. 'I really don't care a damn either way.' He stood up and Carrie was surprised at the anger surging in the depths of his dark eyes. 'Do what you please!' he snapped.

He walked away. She heard him clatter up the stone steps to the bedroom. Carrie poured herself more coffee, disgusted with herself for being so irritable. She'd had a bad night, dreamed of strolling on warm sands hand in hand with Alex, then she'd been woken by those maddeningly noisy bikes, everything had crowded in on her and bitter-

ness had set in from the time she had stepped out
of bed. Her ankles itched, and what was she doing
here anyway? she'd furiously asked herself.

The smell of fresh coffee had tempted her downstairs and she had dressed quickly in shorts and T-
shirt. He wasn't being fair, bringing her to this
lovely old house, expecting her to act as a surrogate
wife and then hauling her back to the Marina to
resume her role as his secretary as if nothing had
happened. And something would happen. She
would fall more deeply in love with him, that was
a certainty. And what was he expecting of these
two days? Her love, her submission? What game
was he playing, expecting her to cook and act out
his domestic fantasies? The shopping list had been
the last straw.

Dismally, Carrie cleared away the dishes and
washed them up. The kitchen window faced out on
to a narrow street that was busy with housewives
shopping, children playing, old men gossiping in
shady doorways. She turned from the sink as Alex
came into the kitchen. He'd changed from jeans
and T-shirt into lightweight narrow grey trousers
and a black Lacoste polo shirt. All trace of the curl
of his hair behind his ears was slicked away.

'Here's a key if you decide to go out.' He put it
down on the marble work surface. 'And here's some
cash if you want to do some shopping. Personal
shopping, I mean. You're right. I shouldn't expect
you to work when it was my intention to give you
a couple of days break from the Marina.'

His voice was noticeably dry and an apology for
her curtness that morning sprang to her lips but he
gave her no space to deliver it. 'There are plenty of

shops and markets in the area, boutiques and shoe shops. I'm sure you'll find plenty to amuse you.'

Was that where he thought her interests lay, in boutiques and shoe shops? She flamed inside.

'Where are you going?' she called out as he reached the front door. She bit her lip as he turned slowly to face her as she stood in the kitchen doorway, a teatowel clutched in one hand, a cup in the other. She knew roughly what he was going to say before he said it.

'You sound just as I imagine a housewife to sound. Demanding!' He lowered his brows and walked slowly towards her. 'I'm going out to pursue my pleasures, if you must know, and, before you ask, I don't know what time I'll be back! See you later, *dear*!'

He lowered his dark head and before she could protest his mouth claimed hers. By no stretch of the imagination could the kiss be likened to one between a happily married couple. It was fiercely passionate, executed greedily and relentlessly and with the deep promise of more to come. It directed every pulse from Carrie's stiffened form directly to her heart, causing a contraction that weakened her legs. She tore her mouth from his, and glared at him furiously.

'Don't rush back, *darling*!' Carrie crowed sarcastically as he turned away from her with a mocking grin playing at the corners of his mouth. 'You won't be missed!' she added under her breath.

He slammed the heavy antique door after him and Carrie's shoulders slumped, but gradually the strength came back to her legs. She rubbed her mouth angrily. Served her right for being such a dimwit as to ask where he was going. As if she cared anyway. Miserably she finished tidying the kitchen.

Resolutely she dismissed that kiss from her mind. It was her punishment for being so irritable this morning. As the heat of it subsided she began to feel sorry for being so grumpy. To make up for it she went upstairs to make the beds. She smoothed the creases from his sheets, lifted the still warm pillow to her cheek. She flung it away from her as if it were ablaze, pummelled it back into shape.

By the time she had finished the beds and changed into a sunflower-yellow sundress for coolness she had convinced herself that she was being selfish. It wouldn't hurt to shop and cook for him. What other boss would have offered her a couple of days' break in his own home? Certainly not Sir Michael, who believed his private life started at six on the dot.

She fingered the peseta notes Alex had left her. And what other boss would leave her money for her personal expenses? She stuffed the money into her purse, knowing exactly what she was going to do with it. Spend it!

Alex's house was in the middle of a busy market area and Carrie wandered the streets and alleyways, enjoying the smells of freshly baked bread, garlic, and sweet jasmine hanging down from roof terraces.

She bought fresh vegetables and salad in an open market in a small plaza. The nectarines were red and sweet, the peaches furry and blushing; she bought both. She found a small café with chickens roasting on a rack behind the counter next to an espresso machine. They'd been marinated in herbs

and spices and smelled ten times better than anything she could have done herself. Safer, too, she
mused as she bought the biggest one; she had been
known to overindulge with some of the hotter
spices.

Already she was loaded with shopping, her arms
aching, the heat weakening every stretched muscle
in her body, but she hadn't finished. Wine. She
bought red and white, not sure of his preference
and not being a wine snob where red and white
meats were concerned. Her last two impulse pur-
chases were a bag of fresh *langostinos*, pink prawns
she would cook with garlic and parsley, and, from
a gypsy vendor, a huge bunch of red carnations.

That was it; she couldn't carry another thing.
Keeping to the shady side of the narrow streets, she
made her way back to Alex's house. She wasn't to
be caught out this time. She had memorised focal
points so as not to lose her way as she had done
the night she had run in to him on the marina
complex.

As she reached the courtyard Alex strode up
beside her. Taking the plastic carriers from her
throbbing fingers, he set them down on the granite
step while he opened the heavy front door.

'Why the change of heart?' he asked, stepping
back to let her pass in to the hallway.

'The shopping, you mean?' She picked up one
of the carriers as he struggled with a folder tucked
under his arm. It slid to the floor as they entered
the kitchen. Building plans slithered over the tiles.
Carrie bent to retrieve them for him.

'Is this the business you came here for?' she
asked.

He took the folder from her. 'I've bought some village houses and I'm having them restored. For my own pleasure, not monetary gain,' he added unnecessarily.

She realised with a cold thud of her heart that he was still in a mood. The morning apart from her had done nothing to soften his bitterness after the row earlier.

'You haven't answered my question; why the change of heart?' he repeated coldly.

Carrie turned from the fridge which she was loading with the groceries, and caught the cold, challenging look in his eyes. Suddenly engulfed with a heat that threatened to take her legs from under her, she grasped at the edge of the work surface. The full impact of what she had done hit her. She had planned a meal, an intimate dinner for two, with flowers and wine, here in his house.

Was she mad? Playing with fire? She had shopped for him, wanted to please him in every way. In every way?

'I . . . I thought it was what you wanted,' she murmured hesitantly.

'And is it what *you* want, Carrie?' he asked, holding her limpid brown eyes with his, reading every terrified thought that was flashing across her brain.

She didn't answer; how could she? They both knew exactly what would happen this night.

'Answer me, Carrie.' His voice was harsh and brutal. He closed his eyes. 'Don't be afraid to admit it,' he went on more gently. 'But don't play games with me; I can't take any more. You know what will happen tonight. We'll eat and drink and then we'll go to bed, with each other!'

Even when he talked this way, so brutally and basically, she loved him. She wanted this night with him, she realised that with a dull beat of her heart. The waiting time he had mentioned that poetical night on her balcony was nearing its end. She had shopped for him today with that sole thought in mind, though it was only apparent to her now.

'Are you really prepared for that, Carrie?' he grated softly.

She nodded, lowering her head, her hair tumbling round her face.

'Well, raise your head and tell me to my face.'

Taking a ragged breath, she jerked her head up bravely. 'It's inevitable, isn't it?' she uttered huskily. 'As inevitable as us crashing into each other in the scented walkway.'

'That's not what I want to hear!' he burst out angrily.

'All right! All right!' she cried back at him. 'I want to go to bed with you. I want us to make love. Yes! Yes! Yes! I want you, so now you know!'

But what he didn't know nor would ever know was that she loved him, a love that would painfully extend beyond this night, whereas his need merely brushed the surface of emotions.

She looked at him only once, a long, painful look, before excusing herself to rest in the afternoon heat, and what she saw in the depths of his dark brooding eyes completely threw her. He was about to realise an ambition he had prophesied. She expected him to show triumph but he didn't. What she read in his eyes was a wariness she suspected was not of her doing, a wariness the love of his life had scarred him with. His ex-fiancée, Fiona, could never have known what she did to him when she had rejected him for his father.

CHAPTER SEVEN

CARRIE would rather have been left to her own devices, preparing the salad in the kitchen, but he had insisted on helping. Alex moved around her, equally tense.

Her siesta had been a disaster. She hadn't relaxed at all. A shower hadn't helped either and though she had taken time doing her hair and dressing carefully she felt a wreck, inside and out. It was all so clinical and so far removed from romance as to be verging on obscenity. Now here she was, preparing a meal, and after they had eaten it . . .

Suddenly she dropped a knife with a clatter on the tiles and the sound reverberated round the stone walls, jarring her nerves horribly.

'Carrie,' Alex said impatiently, 'go out to the patio and I'll bring you a glass of wine.'

'I'll drink it here,' she told him quickly. 'I still have things to do.'

'You've already washed the lettuce three times, sliced far too many tomatoes and I do believe that chicken was roasted when you bought it.'

She forced a grim smile. Had she really doused that lettuce to near death? It lay in a bowl, lifeless. She had. Was it any wonder with her emotions knotting tighter by the minute?

He uncorked the wine while she got two glasses from the cupboard. They went out to the patio

together. Carrie poured the wine with trembling
fingers while Alex lit a candle in a glass bowl on
the table. The night was hot and humid and Carrie
had made the mistake of wearing her emerald silk
dress; it clung hotly to her, piling more misery upon
her.

'The dress suits you,' he complimented as if
knowing she was thinking about it. What a knack
he had of doing that, voicing her thoughts and
moods for her. He knew she was nervous now, and
he must have heard her moving restlessly round her
bedroom this afternoon, like a prisoner preparing
to be shot at dawn. But she was only going to make
love with the man she loved; she wasn't going to
die because of it.

'Why are you frowning?' he asked unexpectedly.
'Don't you like the dress?'

Carrie smiled. 'Yes, I do, but I was thinking of
something else.'

'Would you like to tell me what you were
thinking?'

So his perception wasn't absolute. At least she
would be left with something.

'No, I can't,' she shrugged. 'Tell me when you
are ready to eat.' She sipped her wine, was glad he
had insisted on it; it was beginning to unwind her.
Was this what she needed, a glass or two of wine
to boost her courage? And should she need that
false courage to love this man?

'I've lost my appetite,' he admitted.

Carrie bit her lip; the thought of eating that
chicken, which had smelt so appetising on the spit
and was now cold sober in the fridge, appalled her
too.

'I went to a lot of trouble...' She trailed off, unable to meet his gaze across the table.

'I know and I appreciate it, but Carrie...' he paused '...you didn't have to, you know.'

'No, it was good of you to be such a considerate employer...' She didn't finish for suddenly he rose angrily to his feet.

'And that's why you did it...' he glared down at her '...to thank me for being a good boss? Dear God, Carrie,' he breathed dangerously, 'did you think for a minute that I was a man, not Alexander Drayton the bloody financier, but Alex Drayton the man, with feelings and emotions and needs?' His hand raked frustratedly through his hair. 'I don't want you coming to my bed because you're grateful. I want you there because you want to be and not for any other damn reason!'

Carrie stared at him wildly, then shook her chestnut head in exasperation. 'What has that got to do with it? I was preparing you a meal, not planning on sharing your bed.'

'Don't be so damned ridiculous!' he stormed. 'That's what all this is about, bed, not food. And now you're scared, aren't you? Wondering how you can get out of it?'

'I'm not trying to get out of it,' she flared back at him. 'You should be happy; it was what you brought me here for, wasn't it?'

'Like hell!' he growled furiously.

'Why, then?' she challenged him, her mouth set grimly.

He didn't answer, just stared down at her with eyes that were black and impenetrable. When at last he did speak it was with that slow deliberation that never failed to unnerve her.

'I don't suppose either of us will ever know now, will we?' he grated rhetorically. He gave her one last withering dark look and then turned on his heel and slammed out of the front door.

Stunned, Carrie didn't move from the tiny green patio. She made no attempt to finish her wine. Two mouthfuls had been enough to cloud her thinking. She didn't understand him. He had wanted her and then suddenly he hadn't. She should be glad of that, because deep inside she knew if they had made love she would have regretted it. It would have momentarily eased the pain of wanting him but in the long run she would suffer more. He didn't love her and never would; that pain outweighed and would outlive any other.

Slowly she cleared the kitchen, covered the food she had prepared and placed it in the fridge. After pouring herself a glass of orange juice she took it and the candle upstairs and sat out on the balcony where the *Dama de Noche* was beginning to perfume the air. The other houses around the courtyard were exuding family sounds; a television blaring, children squabbling and laughing, a flamenco guitar being practised with repetitive chords that surprisingly didn't grate on her nerves, shot as they were.

'I'm sorry, Carrie.'

His voice came from the open french doors of his bedroom. Carrie started with shock, so deep in her own depressing thoughts that she hadn't heard him come back into the house.

'You don't need to apologise,' she told him softly, the calmness of her tone belying the pounding of her heart.

'It was a mistake bringing you here. My intentions were all wrong.' He was leaning in the doorway, looking ahead, not at her.

'You did intend to...' She faltered, not able to bring those cold words to her dry lips.

'Seduce you, make love to you, tempt you into my bed? Yes, put it whatever way you like, it spells out the same thing.' His voice was deep and sombre and something else that Carrie recognised: regretful. Was he wishing she were Fiona or even Adela, anyone but Carrie Sutherland, his very naïve secretary? 'And you would have let me, wouldn't you? For any number of reasons but the right one.'

'And what is "the right one"? she asked blatantly. 'Or is this one of your riddles again? Am I expected to know what you are getting at?'

'If you don't, I can't force it out of you,' he murmured.

She didn't understand him, not one bit. He had known that tonight his waiting would be over but now he didn't want her, for some strange mysterious reason he didn't want her. Rejection stabbed cruelly at her heart. What had changed his mind? Or was he one of those men who took masochistic delight in manipulating women to the point of submission and then turning them away at the bedroom door?

Carrie stood up and smoothed down her dress, deciding that enough was enough. She wasn't going to allow him to shred her emotions any further. One thing she mustn't lose sight of—her position. Position? she thought despondently. After this disastrous trip to Cordoba she wouldn't have one! Whether or not she submitted to him would amount to the same thing: the termination of her employment.

'I'm going to make some tea; would you like some?' she asked brittly.

He exuded a hiss of disbelief, eased himself off the door jamb and came along the balcony towards her. Carrie backed away and Alex stopped, held up his hands in defence.

'No, I'm not going to touch you, Carrie, but tell me how you can think of tea at a time like this,' he said acidly.

'I'm thirsty...' she husked, her voice so dry it proved her point.

'So am I. But I can't stay in this house with this atmosphere between us.'

'I'll move out, then,' she blurted. Suddenly tears stung the back of her eyes. It was getting painfully worse. Now he wanted her out, couldn't stand her a minute longer in his house. 'There must be a hotel close by... No, Alex!' He'd moved towards her, purposefully, and she wasn't going to be able to stand it.

He gathered her in his arms and reluctantly she swayed into him. He made no attempt to kiss her and for that she was grateful, oh, so grateful. All would have been lost if he had.

'I've been unfair to you, Carrie,' he whispered into her hair. 'We'll go back in the morning, back to the Marina.'

Tears swelled in her eyes as his hand caressed her hair as if he were consoling a child or a poor hurt animal. For a brief moment she yearned for Adela's cool sophistication—she would know how to cope, but Carrie was lost in a flood of tears.

He held her away from him, gently by the shoulders. His eyes were black, unreadable in the only light from the flickering candle. His hand came up and thumbed the tears from her cheeks. 'Don't cry, Carrie. We're going out, away from here; we can't stay.'

She wished he had never brought her in the first place. It had been so terribly unfair. This was one of his homes and she wasn't a part of it and never could be.

Shaking her head, she refused to look up at him. 'I don't want to go out. You go——'

'And leave you here on your own? No, I couldn't and I won't. Carrie, I'm regretting this as much as you are, but let's make the most of it. There's a restaurant close by.'

Make the most of a bad mistake; the idea was so stingingly painful that Carrie wanted to cry again. She despised him for what he had done to her emotions; bruised them so badly that they ached. He had made her love him, and it had been a game to him; now he didn't want her after all. She didn't want to go out. How could she eat? But the alternative was to stay here in this lovely old house with the scent of the *Dama de Noche* driving her memory pulses wild, reminding her of his kisses and his touch that drove her insane.

'Yes . . . yes, we'll go out.' She moved quickly, pulling away from him.

They went as they were, swiftly, as if the house were on fire and they had to run for their lives. To

stay would have invited the worst disaster; a touch,
a whispered word that would have ignited that
deadly flame till only their fulfilment would have
extinguished the fire.

Carrie didn't bother to take her bag, a comb or
a lipstick, so eager was she to be away from that
fiery temptation. Alex was wearing black narrow
trousers and a black silk shirt that rippled in a flush
of hot air as they stepped out into the courtyard.
He looked wonderful and dangerous and Carrie
didn't know how she was going to cope.

I'll get drunk, she determined as they crossed the
courtyard, Alex acknowledging the greetings from
his Spanish neighbours whose houses were opened
to the warm night. They turned into the narrow
street, past his car parked hard up against the wall.
I'll need to get drunk to get through the night, she
thought desperately.

Alex took her hand as they walked through the
streets. Carrie didn't snatch it away, understanding
the need; he would lose her if he didn't hang on.
The streets were crowded—Spain came alive at
night. The lovely old city was swarming with
tourists from all nations.

They reached the restaurant, down yet another
narrow cobbled alleyway, and went inside, Alex still
clutching her hand. It wasn't a sophisticated place
and Carrie was relieved. She wasn't dressed for it;
her dress, though of silk, was simple, a fitted bodice
with fine shoulder straps, the skirt soft and swirly
round her knees. Her shoes were green strappy
sandals with high heels. She wanted to kick them
off now; they cut into her instep.

The basement was hot and smoky and so noisy that Carrie tightened her grip on Alex's hand. It was crowded but a waiter led them to a table that had just been vacated on the edge of a small dance-floor.

'What do you want to eat and drink?' Alex asked, leaning across the table to make himself heard over the noisy chatter.

Carrie shook her head. 'I'm not hungry; a glass of wine will be enough.' She was glad they were here—though it was rowdy it was better than sitting with Alex in that emotive house.

Alex spoke rapidly to the waiter while Carrie gazed around her, striving to summon some interest. Once again this wasn't the sort of place she'd expect Alex to frequent. He'd been here before, of course; he'd known the way through the labyrinth of narrow streets and cobbled alleyways. The clientele was mainly Spanish with a smattering of tourists; not the rough sort that gave their countries a bad name but people genuinely interested in the country they had chosen for their vacations.

The wine arrived, chatter quietened and flamenco started. As the pace quickened the crowded basement reverberated with the discordant clapping that was so conducive to the flamenco.

Carrie watched in fascination, her interest caught. She sipped the wine, completely unaware of Alex's concerned eyes upon her. The group were gypsies: three weathered men lost in the rhythm of their classical guitars, and two dancers, neither in their youth. The male dancer, a narrow black-haired gypsy in tight black trousers, shirt and broad cummerbund, was intense and dramatic. His female partner, a mature, raven-haired beauty in frothy ruffles of yellow and gold, was stern, yet her every action was strikingly fluid and beautiful.

It seemed to go on for ever, the feet stamping, swirling, clapping and singing. Occasionally Carrie glanced at Alex, sometimes catching him watching her, gauging the effect it was having on her senses. She looked away quickly at those times, not wanting him to look so deeply into her, perhaps guessing how aroused she was by these passionate people.

Suddenly the flamenco was over but the guitarists stayed, now playing a Sevillana, a more formal dance. Several young couples, not professional dancers but diners, were soon engaged in the swirling pattern of dance, arms raised like toreadors, feet stamping but less dramatically than the flamenco.

'Have you ever tried the Sevillana?' Alex asked, moving the wine glasses so that the waiter could put down dishes of chicken in wine sauce, salad, and Spanish rice.

'No, have you?' She looked at the food which Alex had ordered in spite of her refusal, and realised she was very hungry. He was beginning to know her better than herself.

'It's a very sexy dance, don't you think?' He spooned chicken on to their plates.

It was, but she didn't verbally agree—she ate quietly and tried not to look at him. The flamenco had momentarily numbed her senses to him, made her briefly forget the pain of the night. Whatever she might think of him, he'd got it right by insisting on going out. There was so much going on that she couldn't *think*.

'What's happening now?' Suddenly the dancers were back and pulling people from their tables, urging them on to the dance-floor.

'A Sevillana lesson, I believe,' Alex chuckled.

To Carrie's horror she was hauled to her feet by the brooding gypsy dancer.

'Beautiful *señorita*, I teach you.' He grinned happily and led her to the floor, clutching her hand so tightly that she couldn't have escaped if she'd tried.

'I can't!' Carrie gasped in embarrassment.

'It's easy and you have the body, yes, a beautiful body.'

She couldn't be angry with his compliments; somehow they weren't offensive. She could be angry with Alex though; he was laughing, thoroughly looking forward to her making an absolute fool of herself.

Carrie wasn't drunk but had sipped enough to loosen her inhibitions, and after all she wasn't the only one on the floor. It was crowded with eager tourists.

Carrie picked up the pattern quickly and then, once sure of the sequence of movements, she was able to concentrate on the feeling of the dance. She arched her back, twisted her head, her hair swishing around her shoulders, her hands rotating gracefully as she raised her arms and spun round her partner.

'You are natural, like a true Andaluz,' her gypsy instructer praised, his jet eyes glittering admiringly.

'Thank you,' she laughed and twirled away from him. She forgot Alex, forgot everything but the pulsing dance.

'Now do you believe my wild gypsy theory?' a voice grated in her ear as the sequence of dance urged them closer together.

Carrie faltered, her eyes widening in shock. Her gypsy partner had disappeared; her new partner was Alex. She didn't know how long she had been dancing with him, hadn't noticed the difference between the gypsy's graceful movements and his. He moved expertly, as if he had been born to it.

She wanted to rush from the floor but he grasped her wrist and eased her back into the sequence. 'Don't run away, we have an audience,' he whispered warningly.

With horror she realised all eyes were upon them; the other dancers had given up, circling them, and because of that she was forced to stay. She bit her lip, and concentrated on the music.

At last it was over and there was wild clapping and fresh carnations falling around them, ironically red like the ones she had bought for tonight. It brought it all flooding back to her; the pain, the torment of her love for this man who had just danced the romantic Sevillana with her.

Her eyes were wide and fearful as he pulled her towards him and with a devilish gleam in those black gypsy eyes of his he kissed her.

He knew she wouldn't protest, not in front of the cheering crowd. He held her so closely against him that she felt every muscle of his body strain against her. His lips, aroused by the exhilaration of the dance, were daring and exploratory, parting hers with ease and expertise. She was shocked into numbness, unable to move at his audacity in kissing her so sensually in front of so many people.

When they finally drew away, their eyes locked for an agonising moment. Carrie didn't understand the dark depth and intensity of his eyes but understood the hopelessness of her own feelings for him. This sophisticated businessman who ate sardines on a moonlit beach, danced the Sevillana like an Andaluz and most of all drew the gypsy from her soul, was the most exciting person she had met in her life. She didn't want to exist without him but she would have to; somehow she would have to pick up the pieces of her fractured heart and go on with her life.

Unbidden, tears of helplessness sprang to her eyes. Alex frowned and reached for her, but she moved away.

She had to get away, to run till she dropped—to get away from him was her only chance.

Blindly she ran from the smoky restaurant, into the alleyway which was just as hot and clingy. The straps of her sandals cut deeply but she only heeded the pain momentarily. She heard Alex's furious shout behind her and sped on, regardless of her physical suffering.

She pushed her way through throngs of people, uncaring that she was arousing curiosity. She stopped on a street corner, looking this way and that in desperation, her mind spinning, her breath raw and ragged in her throat. Where was she running to anyway? She had no money if she found a hotel, all her clothes were at Alex's...

A group of youths circled her, laughing and making animal noises that had her clutching her ears to shut out the sound. One of the youths caught hold of Carrie's arm and then Alex was there; like a black panther he descended on his prey from what seemed like a great height. The youth went sprawling back into the wall of his friends who jokingly manhandled him and with more shouts of laughter they staggered off down the street.

'Alex!' Carrie clutched at her throat. 'You...that wasn't necessary....'

'You could have dealt with them, could you?' he grated sarcastically, his eyes dark and furious. He grasped her violently by her upper arm and started to march her down the street.

'And where the hell do you think you're running to and from what?' he asked her, so furiously that she was afraid to answer.

She had to trot to keep up with him. His grip was merciless and unrelenting. He was determined to keep a hold of her and she sensed she would do more harm to herself if she tried to escape.

At last she saw his car ahead and the archway to the courtyard. Her heart pounded fearfully as he flung open the door of his house. As soon as she entered, staggering over the threshold, he locked it with such precision that she swung on him, eyes widened like a trapped animal. She realised she still had a red carnation grasped in her hand and clutched it to her heart as if it might save her.

Alex flicked on the candle lights. His chest was heaving, and his voice husked dangerously as he grated, 'Remember what I said in your apartment?

If you were my woman I'd keep you under lock and key...' He didn't finish.

Carrie's eyes flickered fearfully. For his own sweet pleasure... He stepped towards her; one step, that was enough. She read the need in the glittering depth of those black eyes. With a strangled sob she ran, up the stone steps, along the gallery to her room, her hair splayed across her face, her skirt swirling around her knees. Desperately she locked her door, as fiercely as he had locked the front door. She leant back against it, clutching her flower to her pounding heart, gasping for breath, her chest pained with the effort.

'Oh, no!' Too late she lunged for the french doors to the balcony. They were open and he was coming towards her.

'Please Alex, don't,' she husked, backing away.

'Don't what?' he grated, stalking her till he had backed her to the carved door again.

She was aware of the scent from the *Dama de Noche*, and his smell too, musky and Mediterranean, and she knew why she had run for her life. She had seen it in his eyes after he had kissed her in the middle of the dance-floor. He wanted her and nothing was going to stop him now.

Flamenco guitar, this time played by an expert, roused something so deeply primitive inside her that every pulse throbbed dangerously. When he took her in his arms panic surged feverishly, reached the stars and started to somersault down to earth, taking with it her resistance.

'Carrie,' he breathed urgently. 'I can't take any more from you. I want you...' His mouth grazed her cheeks harshly.

'You don't know what you're saying.' She parted her lips in a gasp as his hands in the small of her back urged her into him. 'You didn't want me before.'

'I want you now. On any terms. We want each other and all the reasoning in the world won't change that. Your need is every bit as great as mine so why can't you put us both out of our misery? Admit it, Carrie,' he urged raggedly. 'Don't be afraid to say you want me as much as I want you.'

A small sob burst from her lips. 'You know that already. I've told you. Why do you keep making me say it?' she implored.

'Because I want it from the heart, from the depths of your very soul.'

Helplessly her hands slid up to his neck, shakily, then, gathering courage, her thumbs pressed into taut muscle as his mouth teased the edge of her lips.

'Yes, I want you,' she admitted at last with a heart-rending moan, leaving no doubt of the depth of that admission. It was hopeless to deny him any longer. She didn't care that he desired her but didn't love her. The need inside her was too overwhelming to deny. She wanted to cry with the pain of it, the ache for him to love her completely.

Her words softened him as if he had been on a knife-edge of suspense in case she refused. His mouth caressed now instead of ravaged. But only for an instant. That sort of power and need couldn't be stilled for long. The heat rose, threatened to engulf them. Carrie's head spun.

Alex groaned helplessly as his hands slid the zip of her dress open, peeled hot silk from her fiery skin and lowered his lips eagerly to her breasts. She bit hard on her lower lip as pain and ecstasy seared through her. Her body tensed unwillingly.

'Darling, I'm sorry, I've hurt you.'

'You didn't,' she assured him, her mouth moving to his unremittingly. She didn't want any restrictions. If she was going to have this night of love with him she wanted it all. Every depth of passion, every raw, savage punishment for loving him.

He drew her down to the bed and she clung to him, her own lips and mouth scoring across his, her own hands working as if programmed by some outside force she wasn't in control of. Her fingers dug deep into his back, down to his waist, urged his hips against hers. She was gasping and crying softly to herself by the time he loosened their clothes.

'Green, I love you, green,' he murmured, as he drew away her emerald dress from her hips and blazed a trail of white-hot kisses across her stomach back to her breasts.

He drew back from her when she lay naked beneath him, removed his own clothes with fluid movements that had her watching him expectantly, her breath catching in her throat. Though they had both seen each other naked before, this was so very different. He was aroused, every muscle taut with desire, the heat from his body melding with hers till they were an inferno of need.

It would have been so easy to lose control, to make love swiftly and urgently to satisfy primeval cravings, but neither wanted that. Carrie was hungry to experience every last pleasure with him

and she knew by his controlled restraint that he felt
that way too.

The heat of their bodies shot the temperature of
the room to its mercury limits. Soft light from the
open french windows, from the courtyard beyond,
shadowed and highlighted their nakedness. There
was music in the room, voices from below, laughter
from a balcony. Neither cared if Cordoba witnessed their consummation. They were in a world
of discovery and sensuality of their own, a scented
vacuum.

Carrie touched and aroused. His strong, wonderful body, the first she had explored so
thoroughly. He groaned and laughed softly and
covered her hand and urged her to retrace her steps.
She learnt quickly, the zones she could excite with
a caress of her fingers, a brush of her lips. And she
learned a lot about herself too. His voyage of discovery reached territories she had never known
existed, ventured into sensitive realms she had been
unaware she had. His mouth and tongue on hers,
his fingers simultaneously tracing her inner thighs
drove her wild till she twisted agonisingly under his
touch.

'My wild gypsy,' he uttered helplessly as her
ragged breathing urged him on to new depths. His
lips and the tip of his tongue crazed a pattern of
fever across her stomach down to her thighs till she
cried out and clutched at his hair and arched herself
against him.

His mouth teased, tantalised, seeking and
finding, unselfish and unrelenting in the pleasure
it afforded her. She twisted crazily against him, the
fire inside her out of control, consuming her,

spiralling her into an unknown world and just when she thought that world was coming to an end in an explosive fireball he drew back from her, rose above her like a phoenix, hesitated for only one agonising second before lowering himself into her.

Carrie had never believed anything could be so beautiful and complete. His breath came harsh and unreal in her ears, her name grated out as if it was his last breath. He moved intensely yet lazily at first, soaring higher and higher like a golden eagle in flight, then he quickened, taking with him Carrie's last impassioned breath.

He gripped her, held her against him, urgently guiding and lifting her with him to seek the thermals. They found them, together, soared with them to the brink of a secret mysterious pulsing world that no one, since the beginning of time, had explained or accurately put into words.

They lay in the darkness, wrapped in each other's arms, oblivious to the heat of the night and noise from outside in the hot courtyard. It seemed that the whole of Cordoba was in that courtyard, singing, talking, drinking wine.

A part of Carrie had closed off, the part that reasoned and analysed. There would be time for that another day, another night. Now she didn't want to spoil this delicious vacuum of languorous spent emotions. Her body, dazed with love, floated as light as a cloud on a summer's breeze.

She smoothed her palms over his chest, felt the heat of his skin, the roughness of the dark hair that spread across his body. She smelt the last remnants of cologne mingled with the after-scent of love, his love smell. The even rise and fall of his chest told her he slept. She lay with her head on his shoulder, mouthed a kiss on his warm flesh and fought a frown on her brow.

Those words, spoken so raggedly in the heat of their passion, had not come from the depth of Alex's heart but from the passion of another. 'Green, I love you, green,' from a ballad written by a peasant poet. She wished, with a dull pain in her heart, that those words had come from him.

CHAPTER EIGHT

THE stillness of the morning woke her. She blinked open her eyes, not expecting Alex to be there, but he was, smiling down at her.

She stretched lazily, smiled, reached up and stroked the side of his face.

'Ouch,' she murmured and withdrew her hand.

Alex rubbed his chin ruefully. 'That bad, is it? I'd better not risk a good morning kiss, then.'

'I'm insured,' she told him with a smile, linking her hands around his neck and pulling him down to her. His kiss flooded her with sweet memories of the night before, her aching limbs a testimonial to the thoroughness of his love.

Love? She banished the word from her mind, let herself go to self-indulgence. His lips on hers, his arms around her slender body, his legs encompassing hers.

Suddenly he drew back from her and groaned. 'Can you hear that? What timing!' He swung out of bed, and padded naked to his bedroom next door to answer the extension phone.

Carrie plumped up the pillows against the head-board and, cross-legged, sat back and closed her eyes. It was Sunday and distant church bells pealed and then there was stillness again. Opening her eyes, she saw sunbeams slant across the rough white walls. She was happy, almost completely but for that thread of doubt that held her so cruelly in check.

If she could have one wish in her lifetime it would be that Alex would walk back into the room now and tell her that he loved her.

Her wish wasn't granted, and was he going to talk forever? She could just hear his voice, its low modulated tone, then laughter and more talk. With a sigh Carrie got out of bed and slipped on a baggy T-shirt that modestly covered her, just. She went downstairs to make coffee; it was obvious by the length of the call he wouldn't come back to bed, well, not in the mood he'd left it.

Carrie tried to distance last night from her thoughts but how hard it was; she could feel and taste his warmth even now, but they would soon be driving back to the Marina and then what? Carry on this affair? A sudden rush of tears welled and she gulped iced water from the fridge to quell them. She busied herself with the percolator, desperate not to think.

'It was your father,' Alex stated, coming into the kitchen, dressed now in a short white towelling robe. 'Thought I was the concierge of some hotel.' He laughed.

Carrie swung to him, wiping her hands on a tea-towel. 'Oh, I hope he's all right.' She went to rush out into the hall to take the call but Alex stopped her with a grin and swung her into his arms.

'I said was. He's gone now,' he laughed, nuzzling her neck.

'What do you mean, gone?' she gasped, trying to avoid his mouth.

'He called to tell you he's going away for a couple of days and not to worry if you get no reply when you ring.'

'But didn't he want to talk to me? And where's he going? Why?'

'He's off to Brighton for an exhibition and yes, he did want a word with you but I introduced myself...' he let out an exaggerated sigh '...well, one thing led to another and soon we were——'

Carrie laughed. 'And you forgot about me!'

His mouth closed over hers in a kiss so deep and wonderful that Carrie nearly forgot the coffee; it boiled over with a splutter, forcing her out of his arms.

'Now, look what you've made me do!' She lowered the gas. Alex slid his arms around her waist as she mopped up the spilt coffee.

'I'm looking forward to meeting your father, he sounds a charming man——' The phone rang again, interrupting him and interrupting the thoughts and hopes that surged through Carrie. Alexander Drayton was looking forward to meeting her father! It seemed too incredible to be true.

He turned her towards him, held her hard against him. 'I could leave that, you know,' he whispered huskily. No mistaking what he would leave it for.

She kissed his lips softly. 'You'd better answer it; if you don't you'll be wondering who it is and I would rather like your undivided attention.'

'Wild gypsy,' he murmured, grazing his lips across hers then drawing away with a regretful sigh.

The tone of his voice was so different this time that Carrie went to the hall. He had his back to her, his head bowed. A hand came up to rake raggedly through his hair—a gesture which disturbed Carrie. He did that at times of stress. Her heart plummeted. Business was a cruel interloper. She turned back to the kitchen but stopped as he went on.

'When did this happen?' he asked gravely, then nodded his head at the reply. 'Yes, of course, immediately. Can you hold the fort till we get back later today? Good, good. Are you sure she's all right?'

Shards of icy fear frosted down Carrie's spine at the unconcealed anxiety in his query. Who was 'she'? Had something happened to Fiona?

He put the receiver down, his back to her, unaware that she was watching him from the kitchen doorway. He raked his hair yet again, his other fist clenched and unclenched.

'Alex, what's wrong?'

He swung so sharply, his eyes glittering so brightly that fear lurched inside her.

'Is it Fiona?' she whispered. She'd never seen him so grave.

'Fiona!' he ground out, staring at her as if he'd never heard that name before in his life. 'Fiona who?'

She'd made a terrible mistake. He didn't even know who she was referring to and she had tortured herself thinking he still cared about her. Her relief was short-lived.

'You sounded so serious . . . I thought . . .'

He shook his head, understanding. 'It's Adela...' Carrie's heart slowed dangerously. 'There's been an accident, a road accident. She and Benson——'

'Howard!' her voice blurted in a rush, and she immediately bit her lip at the look on Alex's face. Last night might never have happened; his eyes now

were so steely black and so lacking in warmth that
a shiver ran through her.

'Yes, Howard,' he drawled at last, the beginning
of a sneer twisting his lower lip. 'And don't look
so alarmed—he's not seriously hurt, a broken leg,
but as they hauled him out of the wreck he was
crying like a baby for you.'

'Me?' Carrie husked.

'Don't try and sound so innocent, Carrie. Who
else should he ask for but the person closest to him,
his lover?' With that he stormed upstairs, leaving
her gasping with shock.

It quickly turned to indignation and she flew up
the stairs after him, found him gathering up his
discarded clothes in her bedroom.

'We aren't lovers,' she told him furiously but
sensed, by his angry jerky movement as he snatched
up his shirt from the floor, that he wouldn't believe
her whatever she said.

'We aren't lovers,' she repeated mournfully.

'I heard you the first time. Get dressed and
packed—we're leaving straight away.' He left the
room in a hurry, pulling the door shut behind him
as if he couldn't bear the sight of her any more.

In a daze Carrie quickly showered and dressed
in a spicy orange cotton dress, belting it tightly into
her tiny waist with a soft leather belt, and letting
her hair hang loose to dry naturally. Alex believed
she and Howard were having an affair. If she told
him the truth about her engagement it would come
out that Howard had been involved with Puerto del
Sol and he would lose his job for sure. He needed
it more than ever now. A broken leg. She doubted
if he had medical insurance; he'd always been bad

at that sort of thing. So was she just going to sit by and let Alex believe the worst of her so that her ex-fiancé wouldn't be out of pocket? She didn't know. She needed time to think.

Howard had been with Adela when the accident happened—whether for business or pleasure she wasn't to know. Maybe Alex did; maybe that was why he had suddenly turned against her. If Adela had been pleasuring herself with Howard he could be jealous.

Slumping to the edge of her bed, she held her head in her hands. Alex's change of mood could be down to any of those reasons.

Grimly Carrie packed, and struggled down the stone steps with her case. She left it in the hall and went to tidy the kitchen before they left. Depression swamped her as she started to clear the fridge.

'Wrap that cold chicken and bring it with us. We won't have time to stop en route.'

She turned to him, eyes brimming with tears. He walked past her to the coffee and poured himself a cup.

'Alex...'

He looked at her then, his eyes coldly inexpressive. 'Don't say a word, Carrie,' he warned. 'I don't want to discuss it.'

'Well, I do,' she croaked, her throat raw with pain. 'A little while ago everything was good then that call came and you hate me.'

'I don't hate you,' he told her quietly. 'I hate myself for being such a fool.'

'Because you think I'm just another Fiona?'

'To hell with Fiona. I never cared for her but I cared for...' He didn't finish, slammed his cup into the sink. 'Leave all this—I have a Spanish woman to look after the place when I'm not here; she'll clear it up.'

He cared for Adela, he had been about to say. Carrie packed up the cold chicken, the fruit and a bottle of water. Like a zombie she stuffed it into her shoulder-bag and, picking up the computer, followed him out of the house, not looking back.

Was the day hotter than ever? Even with air-conditioning it was miserably uncomfortable. Two hours, or was it three or four they had been driving? A droplet of perspiration trickled down the side of her face and she reached into the glove compartment for a tissue.

'What's this?' She drew out a package.

Alex coughed, shifted uneasily in his seat. 'I bought it for you in Cordoba. I forgot it was there. You'd better take it.'

Pulses beating dully, Carrie slipped the tissue from a book of poetry. Selected poems by Federico García Lorca. The cover blurred before her eyes. How could he be so cruel and heartless?

The book fell open in her hands at the last page in the world she wanted to read. It was as if destiny had decreed it, as a last poignant stab at her for being such a fool as to think this man had one iota of feeling for her.

> *Verde que te quiero verde.*
> *Verde viento. Verdes ramas.*

She read through a mist of tears. She blinked, then closed the book with a snap. Of course there were several different versions of the translations of

Lorca's poems. Alex had used two. Making love to her he had used the one she preferred not to think about. Green, I love you, green. *Verde que te quiero verde* also translated to 'Green, how much I want you, green,' and that was far nearer the truth. He had *wanted* her last night, not loved her.

'I was never much struck on Lorca,' she told him spitefully, the need to hurt back overwhelming. 'As far as Spanish poets are concerned I prefer Diego.'

'You won't want this, then.' With a movement so swift that she couldn't prevent it he snatched the book from her lap and flung it out of the car window.

It flew in the air as if it had wings, and somersaulted down a ravine, pages flapping wildly.

'That was a wicked thing to do with a book.' The tears brimmed but she swallowed them hotly.

'Perhaps some peasant will appreciate it more than you do,' he snapped back, his last words for a very long time.

'There's the hospital,' Alex indicated out of his window a kilometre before the Marina. 'I'd drop you off but I don't want to hang around. I have calls to make. You can come back in your own car.'

'Don't you want to see him?' she asked.

'I'll see him when he's sober,' Alex bit out.

'W... was he drunk?' She guessed it was a strong possibility.

'Had to be, didn't he? No one goes off the edge of mountain roads at three in the morning unless they are.'

So it was hardly likely that Adela and Howard had been working at that hour. So Alex had reason to be jealous of Howard and if Alex believed she was having an affair with him he'd think she was jealous too but he didn't; he had no regard for her feelings whatsoever.

'And Adela?' It was the first time she had asked about her. She felt no concern for the woman, not because she didn't like her but because whoever had called to report the accident had assured Alex that she was all right.

'She's at home. I'll go straight there from the Marina.'

Carrie didn't even care where 'there' was. Alex couldn't wait to get rid of her to go flying to Adela's side. He'd denied he was having an affair with her yet he'd sounded so concerned over the phone and had turned on her from that moment on.

'As soon as you've seen Benson, get back to the office. With him and Adela out of action there'll be extra work.'

And of course the smooth running of Alexander Drayton's financial empire was top priority. Well at least she still had a job, till she chose to terminate it, and that wouldn't be very long, not long at all.

'Howard?' Carrie was loath to wake him but the doctor had said it was all right to do so. Alex had been right. Howard had been drunk and that was why the hospital hadn't set his leg yet. Mercifully it was his only injury.

'Carrie?' he breathed, his eyes opening fully. 'I thought you were in Cordoba.' He tried to ease himself up but fell weakly back against the pillows, the effort too much for him.

'I was till someone phoned Alex to tell him about the accident.' She pulled a chair up and sat by the bed.

'Did Adela ring?'

'No, someone else, I don't know who. Alex didn't say much, just that you were asking for me. That seemed to be enough for him,' Carrie told him ruefully.

Howard attempted a chuckle. 'I told you he fancied you, Carrie—you'd better watch out.'

Too late, she didn't say. 'Don't worry, I know what I'm doing.' Understatement of the year.

Howard's pale brow knotted. 'What do you mean, he said I was asking for you?'

Carrie shrugged. 'Said you had broken a leg and were crying like a baby for me. I don't know whether to be flattered or not.' She laughed, trying to make light of it.

'Sorry to disillusion you, sweetheart—I know I was a bit tight but I've no recall of calling out for anyone.'

'Maybe you lost conciousness on impact; murmured my name as you came round.'

'Hardly. We only bumped off the road and hit a dumb olive tree. I smashed my leg on the steering column and Adela didn't even hiccup. She walked to a *finca* nearby and got help.'

Suspicion stirred inside Carrie. If he hadn't called out for her, why had Adela said he had? Unless of course she was stirring trouble for her in Alex's eyes. She had warned Carrie before she had left for Cordoba and hadn't Alex said that she was jealous? What better way to break them up, to make Alex believe there was something between her and Howard? But there was no smoke without fire.

'Howard, does Adela know that you and I were once engaged?' How else would Adela get the idea to link the two of them?

Howard stirred restlessly, winced as he tried to move. 'I might have mentioned it,' he said through clenched teeth.

Carrie got the strong impression he was faking his pain. The doctor had assured her on her enquiry that he wasn't suffering in any way; they had given him pain-killing injections. She knew Howard of old, knew his reactions when he was in a tight corner. He'd play for sympathy.

'I thought you didn't want anyone to know we had known each other before?' she persisted.

'It just slipped out some time. I can't remember,' he snapped back.

'It couldn't have just slipped out, Howard. You were adamant that you didn't want it known and then you tell the one person closest to Alex. That sounds ridiculous to me!'

'I'm a bit delirious—don't know what I'm jabbering about.' He closed his eyes as if keeping them open was just too much to expect of him.

'Howard, you're not involved——?' She didn't finish, for a doctor and nurse appeared at the bedside. It seemed to Carrie that Howard looked relieved at their sudden arrival, and it had nothing to do with his injured leg.

She bent over him, kissed his forehead and asked him if there was anything he needed. He shook his head and Carrie left, promising to visit the next day.

She drove back to the Marina wondering where everything was going to end.

'Good trip to Cordoba?'

It wasn't a pleasant enquiry but one sarcastically delivered and meant to hurt because Adela must have known what she had done.

Alex had been awful to Carrie since their return the day before, making it painfully obvious that she was merely his secretary and he was very much in charge.

Only half an hour ago he had hauled her up in front of Howard's relief, Martin Prescott, reduced her to tears by pointing out an error in the sales figures that in fact Howard had made before the accident. She had rushed from the room, distraught and embarrassed, and now Adela was goading with her sabre-edged tongue.

'Delightful,' Carrie murmured non-comittally, and bent her head to the stack of contracts which Adela had just tossed on her desk. It had been a good week for sales.

'Go straight in; Alex is expecting you,' she added politely without looking up.

At least Howard was on the mend—Carrie had phoned the hospital and Howard had been operated on the night before and was well. He would be back to work in about a month's time, sadly too late to entertain the Japanese contingent whose arrival was imminent.

Carrie's head throbbed as she studied the sales contracts and *escrituras* Adela had handed to her, each one in duplicate, Spanish and English. Adela prepared the *escrituras*, the title deeds of each property sold, and handed them to Alex for approval. Normally Alex would have nothing to do with this side of the Marina business—it was Adela's domain—but as everything within the company was in its infancy Alex insisted on following every department through.

This time, so involved with other business was he that Alex had off-loaded that job to Carrie. She wished he hadn't. Legal translation was something else.

Carrie sighed in resignation; at least while she was battling through them she had little time to think of anything else.

Adela came out of Alex's office, laughing brightly.

'Sounds wonderful; dinner at Las Farolas will be just perfect,' she trilled as she pranced out of the office, giving Carrie a sideways look of triumph.

Was it Carrie's imagination, or was Adela's accent just a trifle heavy? Accents could be sexy delivered in a low husky voice. Adela had it off to a fine art. She had Alex back too. The thought was so agonising to Carrie that she felt sick.

'Carrie, come into my office for a minute,' Alex ordered when Adela had disappeared.

Running her tongue over her parched lips she got up, slid the *escrituras* into her desk drawer, locked it, smoothed down her linen skirt and followed him into his office. He closed the door behind her, like a gaoler in a death cell.

Carrie had never felt that way before, as if she was trapped. The last twenty-four hours had withered her confidence to nothing. Alex had been brusque to the degree of rudeness, undermining everything she did, finding fault, even criticising the coffee which was none of her doing. She had put up with it only for one reason. She wanted to make sure Howard was all right before she exploded and told Alexander Drayton exactly what he could do with his job!

'Carrie, I owe you an apology for bawling you out in front of Prescott.' He stood with his back to her, looking out of the window, not able to face her.

She told him, 'I think if you apologise to me you might at least face me. I would think that a common courtesy.'

He swung to her, eyes black and piercing. 'You do, do you? Since when have you told me my job?'

'It has nothing to do with "the job". It's a case of politeness from one human being to another—or is your opinion of me so low that you think of me as less than human life?'

His hand, the stress hand, came up to his hair, raked through it frustratedly. 'You're right, of course—when are you ever damned wrong?'

'I was wrong half an hour ago,' she told him coldly, her chin tilted defiantly. 'Those figures were wrong——'

'They were wrong because of an oversight on Benson's part.'

'They were wrong because I hadn't checked them out——'

'You can't be expected to do everything——'

'That's what I'm paid for——'

'Stop it, Carrie!' he bellowed furiously, coming towards her as if physical violence was the only way to stop her. 'This can't go on.' His voice dropped several octaves and he gripped her shoulders fiercely.

She didn't want that, any contact with him whatsoever. She tried to shake free but it was useless. Her dark eyes, loaded with pain he had caused, warred defiantly with his.

'We can't go on like this, Carrie,' he emphasised brutally.

'I don't know what you mean,' she said strongly though what she felt inside was chaotic. Even clutching her shoulders in anger he managed to rouse every nerve-ending to erotic status. She didn't know what she wanted: a stand-up fight or for him to enfold her in his arms and make love to her. How could love and hate stroll hand in hand in the depths of her being?

'I don't know how to handle this, Carrie,' he told her desperately. 'For the first time in my life I'm in a position that I'm not in control of.' He released her so suddenly that her shoulders slumped.

He turned away and it was in that moment that Carrie nearly weakened. She loved him so desperately, so completely that she was tempted to blurt it all out, but if she thought she was suffering pain now it was nothing to what a confession like that would inflict. He might laugh and deride her, or, worse, feel sorry for her. She wouldn't be able to handle pity. It was that thought that urged her on.

'I think I understand what you are trying to say,' she told the back of his neck bravely. He was trying to let her down lightly. Their night of lovemaking had shown her feelings for him and now he was feeling guilty for his own lack of emotion. Pride rallied her. He would never know the depth of her love for him. 'What happened in Cordoba was very pleasant——'

'Very pleasant!' he echoed, swivelling back to her on the heels of his shoes.

Undeterred, though her heart was breaking, she continued. 'Yes, it was a nice change. It's over now and I think we ought to put it where it belongs, in the past.'

His eyes darkened so dangerously that Carrie took an involuntary step back.

'Is that all you can say?' he thundered.

Courageously Carrie drew breath, clenched her small fists at her side and said coolly and calmly, 'No, there's more. Thank you for taking me to Cordoba, Alex. I'm very grateful for your consideration in giving me a break.'

She walked out of his office, angry with him for the last shot of black fury his eyes had lasered her with. Alexander Drayton couldn't stand not having the last word.

Soon afterwards he stormed out of the office, taking his briefcase with him so that she knew he wouldn't be back. He didn't say goodnight or even look at her, and why should he? Carrie convinced herself. She was history; Adela Carmen Rivera was once again the future. She hoped they both choked on their supper tonight at Las Farolas.

Carrie had planned on visiting Howard after work but phoned the hospital instead. She didn't feel so guilty when they informed her he was sedated. She would go tomorrow.

The thought of returning to her apartment was another depressing idea she shied away from. There she had a choice of reading or sleeping; she felt incapable of either. So there was nothing left but work.

She took the contracts and *escrituras* from the drawer and settled down. It was boring and an hour later she stretched lazily and decided she fancied a coffee. Halfway down the corridor she stopped in her tracks, turned round and hurried back to her office.

She hadn't been wrong; her eyes hadn't deceived her. Two *escrituras* and two sales contracts for the same property had been issued by Adela, both made out to different people.

Not another mistake she was going to get blamed for! Carrie turned to the computer and called up the information she required. The deposits and final payments had gone through in the name of one of those people on the documents but the other name, a company in Denmark, wasn't recorded at all.

Carrie reached for the phone to check with Adela, to ask the reason why she had issued two sets of documents for a single property, the property in question one of the most luxurious and expensive villas they had for sale.

Cursing herself under her breath for being so stupid, she slammed down the receiver. Adela was out with Alex by now. She'd have to wait till the morning.

It wasn't till an hour later, when she was just about sick of the sight of official documents, that a thought crossed her mind. Nothing to do with what she'd been doing—but unconsciously she had been thinking about Howard.

Turning back to the computer, she started going through the personnel files. She brought up Howard's and seconds later gasped with shock.

'That's not possible!'

It was. A mini history of Howard swam before her shocked eyes. There was the usual, a personal profile and details of previous employments, but the one that had evoked such surprise in Carrie was the details of his work with Puerto del Sol!

So Alex knew that Howard had worked for them! But why had he employed him when he knew he had worked for that corrupt company?

Impulsively Carrie brought up Adela's file. If she thought Howard's was a mini history, Adela's turned out to be an autobiography! It was so detailed that Carrie read it compulsively. It even went so far as to list her previous lovers!

Carrie switched off the computer, and sat numb and shocked, trying to find answers. Why should Alex keep such a detailed in-depth file on the one person in the company who should be above suspicion: the company lawyer?

Rubbing her forehead, Carrie wondered how suspicion came into her reasoning. But it was a bit of a mystery. She yawned widely—a mystery it would have to stay till the morning when she would make a phone call that might unravel the web of intrigue Adela and Howard and, yes, Alex had woven around themselves.

CHAPTER NINE

'I'D LIKE to visit Howard this morning, if you don't mind,' Carrie asked as soon as Alex stepped into the office the next morning.

He was late and Carrie had been able to make her phone call, which had turned out to be very interesting but scary all the same. Her heart had been in her mouth in case Alex walked in and caught her.

'Can't it wait till after two?' he crisped.

He looked tired and strained and Carrie wondered if the night with Adela was the cause. Her heart thudded at the thought of what she knew and how it would affect Alex when he found out. Of one thing Carrie was sure—she wasn't going to be the one to tell him.

'It could, I suppose.' Carrie bit her lip and stacked his mail on his desk for him while he poured a fruit juice from the bar. She didn't want to wait till then. What she had to say to Howard was bursting to come out.

'Do you want a drink?'

'No, thank you,' she replied politely without looking at him.

'Why so pale this morning? Had a sleepless night worrying about your boyfriend's condition?' The inflexion in his tone was sarcastic.

She looked at him then, flashed him a look of sheer derision.

'I've told you before, he's not my boyfriend but he is one of the company employees——'

'And as my secretary you feel duty bound to look after his welfare, do you? I'm already doing that, paying his medical fees.'

'Why should you do that?' she iced, suspecting his motivation was money, to get his talented sales manager back selling as soon as possible. 'After all, he was drunk and he was with Adela and they were hardly talking business at three in the morning on an isolated mountain road, were they?' She hoped that hurt and was disappointed when he smiled.

'My, my, we are the little bitch this morning, aren't we? A jealous one too——'

'Me, jealous!'

'You want the lot, don't you Carrie? You drop your fiancé in England for Howard——'

'I did no such thing!'

'You even went so far as to seduce me out of my mind and now you are losing sleep because Howard appears to have turned his affections to Adela.'

'Who seduced who is debatable and I don't care a damn about Howard and Adela, but you obviously do!' she retorted. 'Don't try and make out I'm jealous when it's you spitting feathers. You couldn't wait to get back to Adela——'

'You couldn't wait to get back to Howard!'

They glared furiously at each other, a muscle at Alex's throat pulsing dangerously, Carrie clenching and unclenching her fist in an effort to stop herself punching him on the jaw.

He broke the thunderous atmosphere before it exploded into a storm. 'Get to the hospital and tell

Benson I want him back in this building as soon as possible. Crutches, wheelchair, Zimmer frame, I don't give a damn so long as his discharge coincides with the arrival of the Japanese.'

Stupefied, Carrie gazed at him. 'You are something else, Alexander Drayton!' she breathed incredulously. 'You'd cripple a man for money, wouldn't you?'

'You know me only too well, Carrie,' was his cryptic reply, and he turned his back on her.

She flew out of the office, grabbing her bag as she went.

On the short drive to the hospital she wondered what to say to Howard. As yet she didn't know how deeply he was involved—the only way to find out was to ask. She hoped she could handle it well enough to avoid one of his flare-ups.

'I can see you're well on the road to recovery. Who brought the flowers?' The room was full of them. Roses and carnations, their combined perfume overpowering the clinical hospital smell.

'The sales team sent some, and Adela, of course. I didn't get any from you, though,' he said sourly.

Carrie ignored his bitterness and produced grapes from her bag. 'I thought these much more macho.' She arranged them in a bowl on his bedside cabinet then perched on the edge of the bed, careful not to disturb the cage over his injured leg.

'Are you having an affair with Adela?' she asked bluntly, though trying to make it sound as casual as possible. She watched his eyes for the tell-tale flicker of deceit she had learnt to recognise.

'No way,' he pouted. 'I'm out of that lady's league.'

'You spend a lot of time with her, though.'

Howard frowned. 'I told you before, it's business—anyway, why so interested? You can hardly be jealous of me and Adela... Ahh,' he nodded knowingly. 'You're jealous of Adela and Alex. From what I hear he's playing the field a bit——'

'Shut up, Howard!' She felt the heat rise to her cheeks and turned to the window to avoid his curious gaze. Adela had obviously been putting her oar in.

'Hit a sore point, have I?' he remarked spitefully.

Recovered, Carrie smiled sweetly. 'Not at all. I have no interest in Alex that way,' she dismissed, wishing she could activate her heart as easily as she could her mouth. 'He's a bit out of my league too.' She pulled herself together. 'Anyway, Howard, I didn't come here to discuss the relationship between Alex and Adela but...' She stopped, not wanting to go on but knowing she must. She gazed down at Howard, thought of all the good times there had been before the rot in their relationship had set in. She prayed he wasn't involved but deep inside she suspected he must be, but how deeply she was yet to find out.

'I've discovered something about Adela and I want to know if you are aware she's——'

'Discovered what? What are you talking about?' His eyes darkened and Carrie was sure then. Howard was on the defensive already and she had hardly said a thing.

'She issued two *escrituras* for one of the villas——'

'So what? I expect she had her reasons. Nothing bloody suspicious about that!' He shifted uncomfortably.

Carrie's heart sank. 'I didn't say there was anything suspicious about it,' she said quietly. 'You made the suggestion.'

Trapped, Howard widened his eyes. 'I didn't mean——'

'Listen to me, Howard. I'm going to tell you what I've found out and when I've finished I want the truth from you. There were two *escrituras* made out for one of the most expensive villas on the complex. I checked accounts and the money has gone through for one of the sales; the other, a Danish company purchase, has not been recorded.'

'We...well, I expect they pulled out!' Howard spluttered.

'They didn't. I phoned them this morning. They've paid, three cheques, one for each stage of the construction, all made out to Adela Carmen Rivera, the Marina del Oro *abogada*. The property has been sold twice, Howard, and you are the sales marketing manager!'

'Don't be bloody ridiculous! You don't know what you're talking about!' His eyes flared dangerously. 'Why the hell didn't you go back to England when I suggested it?'

'Is that why you wanted me to go—as I'm Alex's personal secretary were you scared I'd find out and expose this horrible mess?'

So Howard was up to his neck in it. Carrie hadn't wanted to believe it; he'd never shown dishonest tendencies before.

'You wouldn't dare!' he threatened darkly.

With a deep sigh Carrie lowered her lashes. 'I couldn't,' she murmured, 'though it's all you deserve. You've been unbelievably stupid. No, it's not for me to tell him the truth, Howard, that's up to you.'

'You've got to be joking!' he exploded. 'That bastard deserves everything that's coming to him.'

Carrie levelled her dark eyes at him. 'It's the only way Howard, and besides...' she faltered.

'Besides what?'

'Alex knows you worked for Puerto del Sol,' she said.

'You told him? You bitch!' He tried to struggle up, but slumped painfully back against the pillows and he wasn't faking it. His colour changed dramatically to a greyish green.

'Howard, are you all right? I'll ring for a nurse.' Carrie slid off the bed.

'No, no. I'm OK. Could do with a drink, though.'

Carrie held water to his lips and after a while his colour returned to normal.

'The after-effects of the anaesthetic, I think,' he uttered weakly.

'Or your conscience troubling you?' Carrie offered. 'I didn't tell Alex about you, Howard. I wouldn't do that but I checked your personnel file and it was all there.' She didn't mention Adela's lengthy file. 'For some reason Alex took you on knowing you'd worked for them.'

'I have Adela to thank for that, I suppose; she knows a good salesman when she sees one.' He spat this out bitterly and Carrie frowned.

'So you did know Adela in the Puerto del Sol days?'

Howard nodded and offered nothing more so Carrie probed. 'Don't hide anything from me, Howard. Why don't you start at the beginning and tell me everything? I've known you a long time and I can't believe you would be involved in anything like this.'

'Yeah, well, when your back's against the wall you'll do anything for money,' he hissed sourly. 'Everyone in this world is on some fiddle or another; why not me? Why should Drayton have it all?'

In that moment Carrie realised the depth of Howard's hatred for Alex. Alex was the success Howard would never be.

'Go on, Howard,' she urged gently. No use being angry with him—she'd find out nothing that way.

'When I first came out here to join Puerto del Sol there were all sorts of angles being worked. I soon learnt how to suss out a certain type of client, one that was greedy enough to buy when offered a discount and slip the salesman a percentage of that discount. We were all doing it. So long as the company kept up sales they could absorb the discounts.'

'A bit short-sighted, though—it was probably what crashed the company,' Carrie interjected.

'What did we care? We were just trying to make as much as we could at the time. Adela was the one who warned me things in the company were getting sticky. She said if I got out quick I'd probably get another job within the company when new finance was found.'

'As the company solicitor she felt her job was safe?'

'Absolutely. Look...' his eyes flared angrily again '...I don't see what all this has to do with you——'

'I work for the company too,' Carrie told him forcefully. 'Go on, I want to hear everything.'

He licked his dry lips before going on. 'When the Marina del Oro was formed and started advertising for staff I was in. I'm a good salesman and Drayton recognised that, but if you say he knew I worked for the other company I wonder why he took me on?' His brow creased into a worried frown as he gave it some thought. 'You don't think that bastard Drayton set me and Adela up?'

'I wouldn't know,' Carrie answered truthfully. 'As far as I know he doesn't know anything about all this.' She had to admit it was strange that Alex had those detailed files on the two of them, though. 'But how on earth did you get roped into this business of selling properties twice? Has it happened before? For how long do you think you could get away with it? One day two lots of purchasers are going to expect to move into the same villa!'

'That would be a spectacle, wouldn't it?' Howard grated with a smirk on his face.

'It's not funny!' Carrie chastised.

'No, it's not bloody funny!' His eyes narrowed and he clutched at Carrie's hand. 'This was all Adela's idea. She was the one that worked it all out. All I did was to pick clients for the phoney second deal.'

'How do you mean?' asked Carrie in a dull voice. She was beginning to despise her ex-fiancé to the point of nausea—already he was trying to shift the blame to Adela when he was equally up to his neck in it. Where was honour among thieves?

'The Danish company were ideal—they only want the villa for long-term investment.' Howard was opening up now, almost boasting. 'They'll never take up residency. They want us to let the villa for them.'

'But how can you let a place that is already occupied?' Carrie couldn't see the point of that.

He looked at her as if she was simple. 'Of course we don't let it—just send them rental for a while to keep them quiet. We plan on doing the same thing several more times, then in six months' time it's hello, Acapulco.'

Carrie mentally calculated how well they would do with Howard's sales talent and Adela's *escritura* fraud. 'You're talking of millions, Howard!' she breathed in amazement.

'Too damned right.' He smiled for the very first time and Carrie thought the anaesthetic must have turned his brain. The way he was talking it was as if he was going to carry on with his dirty dealings as soon as he could get out of the hospital.

'You idiot, Howard! How could you be so weak? Is it worth the risk of getting caught and probably going to prison in a foreign country? You must be out of your mind!'

'You don't know what it's like, Carrie!' he grated bitterly. 'Being without a future.'

Carrie's hand went to her forehead in exasperation. 'Don't start that again, Howard. No court in the world will listen to your whimpering about what it's like being out of work.'

'Try it some time, Carrie, then you'll know how soul-destroying it is!' he bit back.

She got up and went to the window. She'd know soon enough just what it was like. Her employment with the Marina del Oro was over. She couldn't go on working for Alex feeling the way she did about him and knowing what she knew, and she couldn't tell him, how could she? He was having an affair with the woman who was making a fortune out of him and if she was planning on running off to Mexico with Howard she couldn't have any feeling for him whatsoever. Carrie didn't want to be around when Alex realised that.

'I want you to tell Alex,' Carrie said, coming back to Howard's bedside.

'Don't be ridiculous!' Howard rasped.

'You must, Howard. What has Alex done to you to deserve this? You said he pays well. He's paying your medical bills, too.'

It pained her to think it, but whatever anyone thought of Alexander Drayton he was a good employer. He didn't deserve this fraud and betrayal. 'You'll get caught, Howard,' Carrie murmured warningly, 'that's a racing certainty.'

He waved a threatening index finger in her direction. 'We'll only get caught if you open your trap, and you won't, will you, Carrie? Because if you do I'll——'

'You don't scare me, Howard,' she told him coldly, picking up her bag from beside the bed. 'If I were in your shoes I'd own up before Alex finds out. He's no fool——'

'He is where Adela is concerned,' Howard stabbed cruelly, giving her a knowing look. 'We've got away with it so far—no reason to think it won't continue. Drayton has a weakness: women. You should know that by now. Don't think I don't know how you feel about him, but you'd be wasting your time if you tell him what you know about Adela and me.' He gave a coarse laugh of confidence. 'You're nothing but a secretary. Men like Drayton use your sort; he'd never believe you. Adela knows how to handle him.'

Carrie held herself in check, amazed at her own strength. That had hurt, deeply. She resolved it would be the last time. It couldn't get worse. 'Goodbye, Howard. I won't wish you luck; you don't deserve it. You deserve another broken leg but I'll leave Alexander Drayton to do that for you!'

She walked out of the hospital and stood blinking in the bright sunlight. Her shoulders sagged, every ounce of fight drained out of her. She'd had enough of it all. She wanted to get back to England and her father and their peaceful existence. She wanted to forget she had ever come here to sort out her troubled feelings for Howard. At the time she couldn't have envisaged all this: falling in love with Alex, Adela's and Howard's crooked dealings, and the terrible, terrible ache in her heart.

Carrie couldn't get a flight till the next day. She would have preferred to go immediately but there was nothing available. So she had the afternoon and the night to get through.

After careful consideration she decided it was work as usual till the last possible moment. If she didn't turn up Alex might come looking for her, and better their exchanges on neutral ground, the office, than somewhere more intimate like her apartment.

'What's it to be, crutches or wheelchair?' he asked as she sat down at her desk.

'If that's a joke I think it's pathetic.'

'No joke, Carrie. I want him back on the crew as soon as possible and a broken leg is nothing to a strapping fellow like him.'

'Tell him yourself, then—it's not my place to.'

The phone in his office shrilled and this time Carrie was grateful for the interruption. With eyes as black as a moonless night Alex swung back into his own office.

'Where are those documents I gave you last night?' Adela asked abruptly. She'd stepped into Carrie's office as stealthily as a cat burglar.

Carrie looked up at the company *abogada* in a new light. She'd never come face to face with a criminal before. Where she had ever got the idea she was beautiful she did not know. She had a hard face, yes, a thief's face.

Unlocking her desk drawer, Carrie handed them to her over the desk and smiled. 'Let me have them back when you've finished; Alex hasn't seen them yet.' No doubt the spare one would be missing when they were returned. Carrie didn't mind; she'd photocopied them anyway!

'Thanks,' Adela clipped, and hurried out.

Had Howard already tipped Adela off that she, Carrie, knew all about their scheme? Was that why she had asked for the return of the incriminating evidence? Probably. The thought so depressed her that she didn't hear Alex call for her.

'Carrie! How often must I call you?' He stood
tall in the doorway, his face drawn, his eyes glittering angrily. 'For God's sake stop mooning about
Benson——'

'That's it!' Carrie leapt to her feet, snatching at
her handbag. 'I don't have to take any more of this.
How many more times do I have to tell you ... ?'
She glared at him furiously. She had nothing more
to lose so he might as well know the truth. Lower-
ing her voice, she told him, 'I'm not having you
accusing me of being free with my love any more,
Alexander Drayton. I didn't leave a fiancé in
England. He was here all the time, working for you.
His name is Howard Benson——'

'I know,' he informed her softly, almost with
relief. Folding his arms across his chest, he leaned
casually against the door-jamb.

It was as if Carrie had been punched in the
stomach. She went very pale, her breath a whisper.
'You ... you know?'

'Adela told me last night.'

Carrie's eyes narrowed painfully. 'You knew and
yet you couldn't resist jibing at me. Is that how you
get your pleasure out of life?'

'No, it isn't. I'm just annoyed that you hadn't
the decency to tell me before. What did the pair of
you hope to gain by keeping that from me?'

A deep flush rose to her cheeks and she shook
her head miserably. 'I didn't see that it was any of
your business.'

'Not any of my business!' he burst out. 'You're
both on my payroll, both key members of my staff.'

'And entitled to a private life as well!' she retaliated. 'Or aren't we? Do you expect to own us body and soul?'

'I expect honesty!'

'I've never lied to you, Alex.' Her eyes appealed to his. She couldn't bear it if he went on thinking ill of her.

'If it wasn't a deliberate lie you bent the truth,' he challenged.

She shook her head again, a deep curtain of hair falling across her face. Impatiently she brushed it aside and levelled her eyes at Alex.

'When I came to work here I was engaged to Howard but I soon realised it was all a mistake——'

'Hold on a minute. I want to hear it all. Start at the beginning.'

'The beginning?'

Alex frowned at her. 'Yes, Carrie, the very beginning. I want to know how you got this job, how you managed to manipulate your way in as my secretary so you could be near Howard.'

Carrie slumped down in her chair and rubbed her forehead. She would have to tell him, not all but as much as she dared. There was still no way she could bring herself to tell him about Adela's and Howard's scheme to defraud but, seeing as he knew that Howard had been employed by Puerto del Sol, there was no harm in telling him what he wanted to know.

'I didn't manipulate my way in. I didn't even know Howard worked here till I arrived. I had to leave my other job and the agency I was with offered me this. I jumped at it because it meant a couple of months on the Costa del Sol. Of course I knew Howard was in the region.' She paused and looked up at him. 'I...I thought he was working...with another company...'

'Puerto del Sol,' Alex said, coming and perching on the end of her desk.

'Yes,' she murmured. 'Howard hadn't written and said he'd changed his job.'

'And we both know why, don't we?'

A hot flush engulfed Carrie. Alex *must* know Howard had been involved in those misdealings.

'I didn't at the time. It was a shock to find him working for you. I didn't tell you he was my fiancé because Howard was afraid you would find out about Puerto del Sol and he'd lose another good job.'

'You kept quiet out of loyalty?'

Carrie nodded. 'I took this job because I wanted to see Howard, because I was having doubts about our relationship. He'd lost a very good job in England and he'd been out of work for a month. I know it's not very long but it hit him badly. It seemed to change everything. He became moody and neither of us could cope with it. It made me think that if we truly loved each other we could have worked things out. When he came down here it drew us further apart. I wanted this job to give me the opportunity to find out for sure if we had a future together.'

'And have you?'

Carrie's eyes widened. 'You know we haven't! I told you it was over. What I said about not knowing myself was the truth.'

'And do you know yourself now?' he asked meaningfully and her mind spun back to that night on her balcony with the gypsy moon silvering overhead.

She stood up. She didn't want to be reminded. Alex grabbed at her arm as she went to rush from the office.

She wrenched herself from his powerful grasp, her eyes glazed with unshed tears.

'Sadly I do, Alex, for all the good it will do me.'

'What exactly do you mean by that?'

'I couldn't begin to explain because you wouldn't know what I was talking about,' she told him bitterly.

'I know more than you think, Carrie. I believe that night you crashed into me in the walkway you decided Alexander Drayton was a better proposition than Ho——'

Her hand came up and struck him hard across the face, stinging her hand but seemingly not affecting him. 'I hate you!' she seethed through clenched teeth. 'You're despicable, not even human!'

He pulled her to him then, strongly, powerfully, remorsefully.

'I'll show you just how human I am,' he grated, his voice raw with anger.

His lips were delivered with such force it knocked the air from her lungs. His punishing kiss whirled Carrie unwillingly into another world where nothing mattered but the longing and the need. She struggled at first, not wanting him to know just how wildly and erratically he crazed her pulses when he touched her, and then she weakened hopelessly, let him draw her down into that dark cavern of confusing love and hate. His hands held her firmly in the small of her back, crushing her hard against him, leaving her in no doubt just how much he desired her.

A sob caught in her throat and she wrenched her mouth from his. 'You're right. You've proved just how human you are, from the waist downwards!'

He released her as if she had been suddenly shot with a live current. His eyes were oddly expressionless, black pools of cold nothingness.

'I thought for a brief moment then I might learn your secret,' he said huskily. 'What exactly keeps your motor running. You talk about me being inhuman. Look at yourself, Carrie. I thought by provoking you then you might admit that you cared about me.'

With a sharp intake of breath she backed away from him. 'More of your games?' she cried wildly. 'You want me to say I love you?' She shook her head from side to side as if in a fever. 'That would please you, wouldn't it? I have you all sussed out now. Since Fiona walked out on you it's your life's work to force women to love you so you can have the satisfaction of walking out on them!' Her eyes glazed and furiously riveted him to the spot. 'I'm walking out now, Alexander Drayton, but rest assured I never loved you!'

She turned then and ran from the room, and didn't stop running till she reached her apartment and slammed the door.

She packed, showered, made tea, drank it, all restlessly, leaping out of her skin every time a car drove past, or whenever she suspected a sound had come from his apartment above. But he didn't come near the apartment block. She knew because at every one of those sounds she had flown to the balcony.

Was she insane? Did she think he would come after her? Why should he do that? She was nothing in his life. And yet those few words spun in her mind, 'you might admit that you cared about me...' It had sounded as if he had wanted her to, but she was wrong. He wasn't sensitive enough.

But he was, she reasoned, reminding herself just what a sensitive lover he had been. And he had been human in so many other ways. The *merendero* on the beach, dancing the Sevillana, quoting Lorca...but she couldn't forget his inhumanity, his cruel expectations of Howard—did he really expect him to hobble back to the office just to finalise that Japanese deal? And Adela, how could he allow himself to be manipulated by her when Cordoba had been so beautiful and complete? Manipulate? No, Adela didn't have the power to do that, not unless he was half crazy for her anyway.

Carrie groaned helplessly and tried to sleep. She had cried herself dry and now her head ached and she was suffocating with the heat. Stepping out of the patio doors, she stood on the balcony. It was dark, midnight, and a full moon hung lifeless in the night sky. There wasn't a breath of air to give relief. Carrie wanted to run, to find freedom from the oppression, to find a cool haven till the morning light.

She slipped on a dress, any dress, it didn't matter, and ran barefoot from the apartment.

She ran till she could run no further, ran till her feet were raw. Then she blindly stumbled down a small flight of clay-tiled steps, reaching out open palms as she fell. The fall brought her to her senses. She lay there, stunned for a few seconds and then she wearily got to her feet. It was over, the pain and the sickness. Her stinging, grazed palms were the purge she needed. She walked back to the apartment, her heart as cold as ice and her brain numb.

She knew she would sleep then. She lay on the bed as she was, crumpled and drained. But sleep gave no expected relief. She twisted and turned feverishly, saw Adela and Alex walking towards her, hand in hand and laughing at her. Desperately, in one last effort to claim him for her own, she flung her arms out to him and screamed his name.

'Alex! Alex!'

'Darling, it's all right. I'm here.' He crushed her to him, his lips pressed hard against her wet forehead. 'You've had a bad dream. It's gone now—you're safe.'

With a deep sob Carrie blinked open her eyes, her fingers clawing through his hair to make sure it was him and not a cruel apparition sitting on the edge of her bed.

'Oh, Alex!' she whimpered. 'I love you; I can't bear life without you.'

He held her close, not saying a word, kissing away the fever from her face.

At last Carrie's head cleared and weakly she pushed him away from her. The bedside lamp was the only light in the room, a soft amber glow that mellowed the lines of worry on his brow. 'I don't understand,' she murmured.

He smiled at her. 'You were having a nightmare. I roused you out of it.'

'But how——?'

'I came down to your apartment to talk to you, not able to believe that you didn't care for me. You were so angry before, so I gave you time to think, prayed that you would realise that it couldn't just end like that. The door was open. You were lying here, thrashing around like a fevered wild gypsy, calling my name.'

Embarrassment flushed her cheeks. 'I...thought I'd lost you to Adela——'

His mouth on hers silenced her, a deep impassioned kiss of such intensity that suddenly all Carrie's doubts floated away. She closed her eyes. 'Oh, Alex...'

'Shush,' he soothed. 'Let me do the talking; that's what I came here for. Can you bear it?'

'I can bear anything with you,' she murmured, and then she tried to struggle up from the pillows, her dark-rimmed eyes wide with uncertainty. 'Oh, Alex...'

He laughed softly, eased her back against the pillows. 'Don't look so terrified, my darling. I can read you, remember? Carrie, I love you. I've loved you from that first moment I saw you, naked and dripping wet and so very embarrassed. From then on I was lost. Cordoba was unbearable. I wanted you so desperately but I wanted your love more than anything. I thought I had it; it was the most incredible night of my life—and then it all went wrong.'

'You threw that lovely book out of the car window. I should have known why you bought it for me.' She touched his cheek and he gripped her fingers, pressed his lips to them.

'I should have made it clearer to you before. I thought you knew, thought you must have known, but you didn't, did you?'

'I must have been blind,' she uttered helplessly.

'You were. I told you in so many ways but you didn't understand, did you?'

'Some women need it spelt out to them.' She smiled ruefully up at him. 'You never actually said the words and then there was Adela...' Her eyes clouded. 'Something's happened, hasn't it?'

'They've gone,' he told her.

He didn't need to say who but he started to say why and Carrie stopped him. 'I know all about it, Alex. The fraud, the deception...'

He raised a dark brow in surprise and she smiled. 'I'm not your secretary for nothing, Alexander Drayton. But I got one thing horribly wrong. I didn't think you knew but of course you did, didn't you? That was why you kept those files on them both. Why you put up with both of them for so long.' Carrie sighed deeply. 'Howard was a fool to think he could put one over on you and I was a fool not to have seen and understood what was going on.'

'Why didn't you say anything to me, Carrie? It would have saved such a lot of heartache between us. Did you really believe I was romantically involved with Adela?'

She nodded. 'I'm sorry for mistrusting you, Alex, but I felt so fragile and vulnerable. Adela was so worldly.'

'Greedy too. She and Howard made a good couple. I knew if I gave them enough rope they would hang themselves. I had to put up with the pair of them because I wanted more evidence, enough to put them out of action for a long time.'

Carrie frowned. 'But you said they've gone.'

'They won't get far with Benson on crutches. They'll probably be picked up at the airport. I reported Adela to the Spanish equivalent of the Law Society some time back. They've been carrying out an investigation into her company. This isn't the first time this has happened; she's as twisted as a corkscrew but no one has had any hard evidence to put her away before. Now with the *escrituras*——'

'I took copies,' Carrie breathed excitedly and Alex laughed.

'Did you, now? I have the originals.'

'Oh.' She looked disappointed. 'I thought I was being so clever.'

'And what had you intended doing with those copies?' he asked her pointedly, and she knew she would have to tell him the truth.

'I . . . I was going to put them in an envelope and leave them on your desk when I went.'

He looked round at her suitcase standing by the wardrobe. 'Would you really have walked out on me, Carrie?' he asked quietly.

She nodded, her lashes glistening with fresh tears. No need to hide anything from him now. 'I love you so much, Alex, and I couldn't bear to think that you didn't love me. I couldn't have gone on working for you. I thought you only wanted me for an affair, and I wanted you for ever. And then I thought you cared for Adela and you thought I cared for Howard and it was all such a terrible mess.'

He reached for her then, pulled her into his arms. 'And all the time Howard and Adela were carrying on behind our backs.'

'Were they?' she murmured into his hair, not really caring how long their affair had been going on.

'Since Puerto del Sol days,' Alex told her, and then dismissed them both from their minds with a deep kiss.

'I love you, darling,' he husked at last. 'Wherever am I going to find another perfect secretary?'

'Are you looking for one?' she laughed in his ear. 'I don't think it's necessary, do you? I was just thinking the job was getting interesting.' Very interesting. His mouth moved urgently against hers and for a moment she lost herself in the deep love that enfolded them.

'What about the Japanese?' she asked as they broke for breath.

Alex let out a ragged sigh of dismay. 'That is precisely the reason I want a new secretary. Now forget the Japanese; I can handle them.' His hands slid her dress from her shoulders, the red dress she had worn when she had run into him in the scented walkway. 'I want to marry a wild gypsy,' he breathed heavily at the sight of her heated body, 'not the perfect secretary.'

'I . . . I'm not a wild gypsy,' she denied in a gasp as his mouth closed over her breast, soaring her temperature, racing her pulse, and forcing her heart to twist passionately, but she knew that he was right, that when she was in his arms with his mouth tantalising hers there would always be a wild gypsy in her soul, but only for him and the green wind beneath a Spanish poet's gypsy moon.

Harlequin Presents ®

is

 exotic

☑ dramatic

☑ sensual

☑ exciting

☑ contemporary

☑ a fast, involving read

☑ terrific!!

Harlequin Presents—
passionate romances
around the world!

WELCOME TO

The quintessential small town where everyone knows everybody else!

Finally, books that capture the pleasure of tuning in to your favorite
TV show!

GREAT READING...GREAT SAVINGS...AND A FABULOUS FREE GIFT!

Each book set in Tyler is a self-contained love story; together, the
twelve novels stitch the fabric of the community. The covers honor
the old American tradition of quilting; each cover depicts
a patch of the large Tyler quilt.

With Tyler you can receive a fabulous gift ABSOLUTELY FREE by
collecting proofs-of-purchase found in each Tyler book. And use our
special Tyler coupons to save on your next TYLER book purchase.

Join your friends at Tyler for the sixth book, SUNSHINE
by Pat Warren, available in August.

*When Janice Eber becomes a widow, does her husband's friend
David provide more than just friendship?*

BIG SUMMER READ

Summer Reading At Its Best

In July, Harlequin and Silhouette bring readers the Big Summer Read Program. Heat up your summer with these four exciting new novels by top Harlequin and Silhouette authors.

SOMEWHERE IN TIME by Barbara Bretton
YESTERDAY COMES TOMORROW by Rebecca Flanders
A DAY IN APRIL by Mary Lynn Baxter
LOVE CHILD by Patricia Coughlin

From time travel to fame and fortune, this program offers something for everyone.

Available at your favorite retail outlet.

BSR

"GET AWAY FROM IT ALL" SWEEPSTAKES

HERE'S HOW THE SWEEPSTAKES WORKS

NO PURCHASE NECESSARY

To enter each drawing, complete the appropriate Official Entry Form or a 3" by 5" index card by hand-printing your name, address and phone number and the trip destination that the entry is being submitted for (i.e., Caneel Bay, Canyon Ranch or London and the English Countryside) and mailing it to: Get Away From It All Sweepstakes, P.O. Box 1397, Buffalo, New York 14269-1397.

No responsibility is assumed for lost, late or misdirected mail. Entries must be sent separately with first class postage affixed, and be received by: 4/15/92 for the Caneel Bay Vacation Drawing, 5/15/92 for the Canyon Ranch Vacation Drawing and 6/15/92 for the London and the English Countryside Vacation Drawing. Sweepstakes is open to residents of the U.S. (except Puerto Rico) and Canada, 21 years of age or older as of 5/31/92.

For complete rules send a self-addressed, stamped (WA residents need not affix return postage) envelope to: Get Away From It All Sweepstakes, P.O. Box 4892, Blair, NE 68009.

© 1992 HARLEQUIN ENTERPRISES LTD.   SWP-RLS

"GET AWAY FROM IT ALL" SWEEPSTAKES

HERE'S HOW THE SWEEPSTAKES WORKS

NO PURCHASE NECESSARY

To enter each drawing, complete the appropriate Official Entry Form or a 3" by 5" index card by hand-printing your name, address and phone number and the trip destination that the entry is being submitted for (i.e., Caneel Bay, Canyon Ranch or London and the English Countryside) and mailing it to: Get Away From It All Sweepstakes, P.O. Box 1397, Buffalo, New York 14269-1397.

No responsibility is assumed for lost, late or misdirected mail. Entries must be sent separately with first class postage affixed, and be received by: 4/15/92 for the Caneel Bay Vacation Drawing, 5/15/92 for the Canyon Ranch Vacation Drawing and 6/15/92 for the London and the English Countryside Vacation Drawing. Sweepstakes is open to residents of the U.S. (except Puerto Rico) and Canada, 21 years of age or older as of 5/31/92.

For complete rules send a self-addressed, stamped (WA residents need not affix return postage) envelope to: Get Away From It All Sweepstakes, P.O. Box 4892, Blair, NE 68009.

© 1992 HARLEQUIN ENTERPRISES LTD.   SWP-RLS

"GET AWAY FROM IT ALL"

Brand-new Subscribers-Only Sweepstakes
OFFICIAL ENTRY FORM

This entry must be received by: June 15, 1992
This month's winner will be notified by: June 30, 1992
Trip must be taken between: July 31, 1992—July 31, 1993

YES, I want to win the vacation for two to England. I understand the prize includes round-trip airfare and the two additional prizes revealed in the BONUS PRIZES insert.

Name _____

Address _____

City _____

State/Prov. _____ Zip/Postal Code _____

Daytime phone number _____
(Area Code)

Return entries with invoice in envelope provided. Each book in this shipment has two entry coupons — and the more coupons you enter, the better your chances of winning!
© 1992 HARLEQUIN ENTERPRISES LTD.   3M-CPN

"GET AWAY FROM IT ALL"

Brand-new Subscribers-Only Sweepstakes
OFFICIAL ENTRY FORM

This entry must be received by: June 15, 1992
This month's winner will be notified by: June 30, 1992
Trip must be taken between: July 31, 1992—July 31, 1993

YES, I want to win the vacation for two to England. I understand the prize includes round-trip airfare and the two additional prizes revealed in the BONUS PRIZES insert.

Name _____

Address _____

City _____

State/Prov. _____ Zip/Postal Code _____

Daytime phone number _____
(Area Code)

Return entries with invoice in envelope provided. Each book in this shipment has two entry coupons — and the more coupons you enter, the better your chances of winning!
© 1992 HARLEQUIN ENTERPRISES LTD.   3M-CPN